Lemon

Stefan Jurewicz

Published by Stefan Jurewicz, 2023.

LEMON

First edition. June 16, 2023.

ISBN: 979-8215847893

Written by Stefan Jurewicz.

For Mike and Meaghan.

AUTHOR'S NOTE

This book is an accompaniment to the songs "Here, Then Gone," "M," and "Playboys & Dishes" by the Desert Island Big Band, dubbed the "Lemon Trilogy" after inspiring the words you're about to read. The songs informed the storyline, which then informed how the songs were presented to the world. I recommend listening to them before you continue.

For your better understanding, there are a few language laws you should know. Most proper nouns follow these laws. Firstly, a person's name will be, at the very least, one capitalized letter, though will typically be found within multiples of its lower case (ex: ggGggg). Pets do not apply, though many people choose to give them human names anyway. Secondly, countries, states, provinces, cities, towns, et cetera all begin with a number, followed by a sequence of characters (ex: 4-/^f-#). Finally, places of business are all lowercase letters, struck through, though brand names do not change, even when named after a person (ex: one can buy Uncle Ben's rice at ~~plim~~).

PART ONE

CHAPTER ONE

Three bottles of Jim Beam, one jumbo bag of salted pretzels, and a single lemon.

Xxxxxxx watched each item pass from the belt to the scanner, then to the bagging area, his hands moving as if independent of the rest of his body.

It wasn't until he reached the lemon that something struck him as worthy of his attention. His focus snapped back to the citrus in his hand, which was now definitively back in his control, and his brow furrowed as he tried to figure out what the hell was so strange about it. He looked over at the rest of the order: three bottles of Jim Beam and a jumbo bag of pretzels, then down at the tiny digital clock on his register. 11:17am. Xxxxxxx chuckled to himself for being so slow, and without looking up, said:

"The breakfast of champions."

She laughed.

"Oatmeal's for suckers."

Caught off guard by her response, Xxxxxxx cackled loudly.

He looked up. In front of him stood a woman he'd never seen before.

0xx-M- was a fairly small town, ten thousand or so, and Xxxxxxx often found himself surrounded by many of the same faces. While it wasn't unusual to see a new one, it certainly wasn't so common that he didn't take notice when one showed up.

She had long, curly, copper hair, and her face was covered with piercings. At first glance Xxxxxx counted six. She was wearing ripped black jeans, a white t-shirt, and a black leather jacket, despite the twenty-plus degree weather outside. She looked to be in her mid to late twenties, the same age as Xxxxxx. When she pulled out her credit card to signal how she'd like to pay, Xxxxxx noticed her hands were covered in tattoos; and despite one hand being partially covered by a homemade bandage, he was willing to bet they didn't end at the wrist.

She bent over the machine to input her pin.

"It's for ~~une~~," she said without looking up. "Boss asked me to run some errands for him."

Xxxxxx nodded. ~~une~~ was one of the only bars in town, and certainly the most popular. He had served the owner, RRr, a few times over the years.

He tore her receipt off as it finished printing, passing it to her with a pen for her signature.

"So, you're new to town?"

She didn't reply right away, wordlessly signing the paper before passing it back to Xxxxxx.

"Yeah," she finally said. The corner of her mouth lifted slightly. "See you 'round then, huh?"

She winked, and Xxxxxx laughed. Something about the way she did it didn't come across as flirtatious, but funny. It seemed to say, "you're alright, kid."

She grabbed her groceries and Xxxxxx watched her black Doc Martens carry her out ~~mins~~' automatic front door. He looked down at the receipt and saw that she had signed it with the letter M.

. . . .

Xxxxxxx grunted as his ass landed heavily in his recliner. His beer sloshed around in his glass and spilled out onto the armrest.

"Ah, fuck."

He placed the glass on the coffee table in front of him and went back into the kitchen to grab a dishtowel. On his way back into the living room he stopped, paused for a moment, and leaned back just far enough that he could see the clock on the microwave. It read 10:26pm, which meant it was actually 10:39pm.

Xxxxxxx had watched that clock slip out of time for years, and now he watched it with a sort of fascination. How far could it slip before the whole unit died? He remembered reading somewhere that digital clocks sometimes sped up because of electrical surges over their lifetime that caused their internal oscillators to work a little faster for just a moment. Or something like that anyway.

He shook his head. Why had he wanted to check the time again? Oh, right. At 10:30pm every weeknight, Xxxxxxx liked to listen to 107.7fm's "Never Heard Of 'Em." Despite the god-awful name, it was a surprisingly great show. A solid hour of music with no interruptions, barring the occasional mention of the artist and title of the next track, and all the music was quite literally from artists Xxxxxxx had never heard of, without fail. It was a highlight in his day to be able to sit down in his recliner, suck a beer, smoke a joint, and listen to something he'd never heard before.

He turned on the radio and returned to his chair after wiping the arm down, tossing the dishtowel on the coffee table next to his beer. He'd caught the show right between songs. The host, ssSs, came on air only to say:

"c&*, Modern Lingo."

Before Xxxxxxx could fully register how ridiculous a band name c&* was, drums swirled in from seemingly underground, and the song broke out into sparkling guitars dancing over dark, distorted drums and bass.

Xxxxxxx put his feet up, took a swig of his beer, lit a half-smoked joint he'd left lying nearby, and exhaled as the vocals came in.

Throw your knife in the river
If it don't cut the way you know it should
You can't stand the modern lingo
The way that you could
Your claim to fame is your lack of interest
And it's treated you well so far
She left a note on the kitchen table

Xxxxxxx marveled, just for a second, at the way the song made him feel. He struggled for a moment to find the right word to describe it, and came up with "exposed." He laughed.

As if this person's life experiences have anything to do with mine, he thought, saying "what an asshole" aloud. He assumed the profanity was directed at himself but had another laugh at the idea that he was secretly mad at the singer. Funny how dangerous a relatable moment can be.

Suddenly inspired, Xxxxxxx shut off the radio and marched toward his office. Dimly lit by only a single antique lamp in the corner, Xxxxxxx's office was sparse, simple. He kept one high-backed beige swivel chair behind a large, black, wooden desk he had found on the side of the road. Partially sanded, it looked like an abandoned DIY project; but there was something elegant about it in Xxxxxxx's eyes. Maybe it was the worn brass detailing, maybe it was its resiliency. Either way, he liked it, so he took it home.

On his desk sat a pad of 8.5"x11" lined paper and a pen. Black ink. The page was fresh, just like he'd left it.

He sighed, leaning just for a moment against the doorframe, before crossing the carpet to his chair. He grabbed the pen and started writing, stream of consciousness, in the hopes of articulating his embarrassing interaction with the radio in some sort of meaningful way. After a few minutes, he stopped.

Leaning back in his chair, he tore the page off the pad and read what he'd written, brow furrowed. His mouth moved slightly, half-following the words on the page.

Not bad, he thought, *but it reads too simply. Where's the worldview? Where's the "ah-ha!" moment? Where's the anything-to-make-anyone-give-a-shit-about-reading-this?*

Frustrated, he balled up the paper and tossed it in the bottom drawer of his desk, which was already bursting with similar pages. As much as he felt like a failure, there was a small part of him that felt his work was worth hanging on to. Maybe he'd go back one day and find something he'd missed the first time. While he wasn't quite sure what that could be, it sure could be something.

Xxxxxxx shuffled out of his office and back out to the living room, where he took another hit, turned on the TV, and turned off his brain.

CHAPTER TWO

Xxxxxxx woke up in the recliner; his t-shirt twisted uncomfortably around his torso. Parts of it felt damp.

That's when he noticed the beer still in his lap. He groaned and was interrupted by a coughing fit. He cleared the phlegm that had built up in his throat overnight, pulled his shirt off, and tossed it across the room, through the open door to his bedroom, and onto the floor inside. He was hoping to get it on the bed, but mid-release remembered it was wet and was happy he'd missed.

After pulling himself out of the recliner and into the bathroom to take a shower, he turned on the water, sat on the toilet seat, and put his head in his hands. He sighed heavily.

Lately, he had been finding his daily routine more and more difficult. There was something so frustratingly monotonous about the whole thing. He was almost thirty now, and all he had ever been was a cashier at ~~mins~~. He often thought about doing something else, but knew nowhere else in town would start him at the wage he was currently making, which was already barely enough to cover his monthly expenses. ~~mins~~ had been Xxxxxxx's high school job, and while it may not have been glamorous in any sense of the word, he *had* worked his way up the pay scale over the years.

The water warm enough, Xxxxxxx stripped and got in the shower.

What a load of bullshit, he thought; yanking at the stained shower curtain his labour had paid for.

He really hated being such a downer all the time. So much so, he had trained himself to point out the positives in any given situation whenever he could. Yet it seemed no matter how he tried his internal dialogue stayed the same: a big, fat middle finger to the world. The irony of the whole exercise was that his superficially positive outlook caused many of the people around him to find his company quite enjoyable.

He had quite a few of what you might call "friends" at ~~mins~~, but he never saw any of them outside the workplace, and certainly had no intention of changing that. Not for lack of wanting company, but rather that Xxxxxxx had a difficult time legitimately connecting with anybody. So much about them seemed so perpetually superficial, as if the first thought to pop in their heads was also the last about any given thing. He craved depth, but at the same time resented his seemingly pompous attitude; often talking himself off the pedestal he'd placed himself on just moments before.

"Fuuuuuuuuuck," he said to no one, pulling the skin down his face with the palms of his hands.

Get over yourself, he thought, shutting off the water.

He dried himself off, pulled on his brown and beige uniform, and started on breakfast.

• • • •

Xxxxxxx enjoyed his drive in to work.

Years ago, he had made the decision to move to an apartment in the east-most end of town as a way of intentionally increasing his commute time.

Not being too urbanized, 0xx-M- still had plenty of forested area, most of which could be found to the east, the less developed end of town. Xxxxxx used this to his advantage as a way of not only avoiding traffic, but also allowing him an extra ten minutes of gorgeous scenery before being stuck inside a supermarket all day.

He pulled into the ~~mins~~ parking lot just in time to see the woman from the day before walking out the front entrance. They locked eyes as Xxxxxx coasted by. She smiled and winked at him, and Xxxxxx blushed.

Jesus, he chastised himself, *what are you, twelve?* He winked back and she laughed. Expecting his self-loathing to skyrocket, he was surprised when he felt no embarrassment at all. It wasn't as if she was laughing *at* him, but rather he had *made* her laugh. There was a line between the two, surely.

He punched in at 12:30pm exactly. As he grabbed his till and made his way over to his supervisor, he couldn't get the image of the winking woman out of his head. He did this all the time and cursed the chemicals in his brain for what seemed like yet another crush.

But it's not a crush, he thought. Not in any sexual way, at least. Sure, yes, he would admit she was a good-looking woman, but his strange obsession was hung up on something else. He wondered if it was the way she dressed. Even today she was wearing the same leather jacket, white shirt, black boots, and ripped jeans as the day before. Her entire image seemed very "anti-establishment."

No, he thought, *that wasn't it either. Maybe it was—*
"Thirteen."
"Huh?" said Xxxxxx, snapping back to the present.
"Thir-teen," said ~~ffF~~, Xxxxxx's supervisor, rolling his eyes.

Xxxxxx bit his tongue, nodded, and winked at ffF before walking over to register thirteen to start his shift. He smiled to himself, wondering if the wink was making a comeback.

. . . .

She didn't come back again until the following Monday evening. Her order was a bit more extensive than the first time, but still contained the three bottles of Jim Beam, the jumbo bag of salted pretzels, and the lemon. A frisson of excitement coursed through Xxxxxx at the prospect of talking to her again. He really wanted to nail down what it was that fascinated him so much.

Suddenly, Ddd, the next cashier down the line from Xxxxxx, and a real turnip of a woman, called out "open on twelve!" and the winking woman bee-lined in her direction. The wind taken out of Xxxxxx's sails, he watched as the woman walked right past Ddd's cash and right up to his. She began unloading her items, straight-faced until Ddd loudly sucked her rotting teeth in disappointment, when the woman lost her composure and had to bite her lip to keep from bursting into laughter.

Xxxxxx on the other hand wasn't quite so in control and cackled loudly, slapping his hand over his mouth a second too late. Ddd huffed noisily and turned her back to them both, clearly not appreciative of the joke.

"Howdy, stranger," said the winking woman.

"Stocking up for another round I see."

"You bet. Cage match, anything goes!"

Holding back laughter, Xxxxxx continued the bit as he started scanning her order.

"In this corner, wearing the white trunks, we've got Jimmy the Beam, weighing two-point-two-five litres—," he said.

"And in this corner, wearing no trunks at all..!"

She wolf-whistled before continuing.

"...We've got M, weighing in at who the fuck cares—!"

"The bell rings and she's pounding 'em back, one after the other—!"

"This is gonna be over real quick, folks—!"

"And just like that—!"

"POW!"

"Jimmy the Beam is down! KNOCKOUT!"

M's face went serious for a moment.

"Hey, thanks. You know, I do my best to dress well, go to the gym..."

Xxxxxxx lost it. He doubled over, cackling loudly. M began to laugh as well, though seemingly more at how the joke was received than the joke itself.

When they'd both collected themselves, Xxxxxxx gestured at the debit machine for M to pay. She slid the credit card and signed her receipt.

"Not much for entertainment 'round here, is there?" she smirked.

"Not really," Xxxxxxx chuckled, wiping tears from his eyes.

"Well, aren't I glad I found you then, huh?"

Xxxxxxx blushed, and she winked.

"Don't you go soft on me now."

• • • •

M would come in every few days, and each time she'd go straight to Xxxxxxx's cash, leaving Xxxxxxx to wonder if maybe she had a thing for *him*. He had never really been what you might call "traditionally good looking," but if you looked at just the right angle, he wasn't a *complete* pile of dog shit.

Considering this, he realized there was a large part of him that hoped their relationship wasn't rooted in romance at all. There was something so effortless about their conversations that the idea of dating her struck Xxxxxx as an unnecessary complication. He liked the simplicity of it all.

As their relationship grew friendlier, Xxxxxx imagined stopping by ~~une~~ to visit her at her place of work.

~~une~~ was something of a staple in 0xx-M-. As one of the only bars in town, it had a sizable regular crowd, but it was more the fact that it had been around so long that gave it what you might call a "legendary" status among locals. It was famously known as "0xx-M-'s first bar," and it didn't need any more than that to solidify its reputation.

Xxxxxx imagined being able to have a conversation that lasted longer than the two minutes it took to scan and process her grocery items. He imagined being comfortable somewhere that wasn't his recliner. What a concept.

* * * *

After another few visits, Xxxxxx finally summoned the courage to ask for her number. He hesitated at first, fearing it might change the dynamic he had come to value so much, but he also knew he was tired of only having friends inside these four walls and wanted some way of differentiating M from the rest of them. She gave it to him without hesitation, and Xxxxxx felt a wave of embarrassment for making such a big deal out of nothing.

He had concluded that it was her quick wit and seemingly impenetrable self-confidence that had snared his interest. She never seemed to think too long before speaking, yet always had the perfect response for everything he threw her way. Her mind worked incredibly fast, and her confidence in that intellect was something Xxxxxxx had caught himself almost looking up to once or twice.

She passed back her signed receipt along with the paper she'd written her number on, and Xxxxxxx slid the latter into his shirt pocket. She winked at him, and just as quickly as she had arrived, she was gone again, leaving Xxxxxxx to himself and everyone else around him.

CHAPTER THREE

M stared at the Chevelle parked in the lot across the street. It was an olive green, and had two thick, black racing stripes on the hood. The tinted window she was looking through made it difficult to be sure, especially now that the sun had set, but she was pretty sure it was a '68.

Beautiful, she thought. *Wrong year though.*

The child in the seat in front of her suddenly and inexplicably shrieked the way only young children can, and M was violently brought back to the present.

She was on a Greyhound bus, stopped at a red light. Beyond that she had no clue where she was anymore. She looked around the lot the Chevelle was parked in for some kind of indication and came up short.

The light changed, and the bus crept forward.

She had gotten on the bus in 7*t*hx*, intending to make it all the way to 3—-rr/l. But with 3—-rr/l being almost halfway across the country the cost of the ticket alone would have drained most of her savings, and she needed to make sure that wherever she ended up she had enough money for food and shelter until she could find a job. 0xx-M- was the best she could do for now, and seeing as it was the Greyhound's last stop, she wasn't too bothered by her unfamiliar surroundings.

Suddenly, a foul odor slapped her across the face. She grimaced and looked down at her ratty clothes. Had she changed them since..?

Fuck, girl, that was days ago now, she scolded herself. She vowed to change them as soon as she found a place to crash that night. Her bag may have been packed quickly, but she was thankful she had at least had the foresight to grab a fresh set of clothes.

The bus pulled into a station and M learned she was in 7u~g$+o~, 9(a. Almost there now. Her eyelids felt heavy. 9(a was a much larger state than she'd thought.

A middle-aged man dressed in an untucked, light blue dress shirt, dark grey slacks, and plain navy tie hanging loosely around his neck, walked onto the bus, dragging his feet all the way to where M was seated. When they made eye contact, he smiled uneasily at her. She was used to that. She debated calling him a "normie," rolling her eyes back into her head, and opening her mouth to reveal a wriggling, forked tongue when he spoke first.

"Hey there," he chimed. He sounded tired, but friendly.

"Hi," said M, before looking out the window again.

Another time, she thought. She wasn't really in the mood.

Her phone had been ringing non-stop since she left. At one point she swore she could have let it go and it would have vibrated itself right down the street, carried away by nothing but the dynamism of attempted contact.

Her voicemail had filled up almost immediately, and as a result the calls had begun dropping off, and she was sure that within a couple more days they would stop entirely.

The middle-aged man triple-checked his ticket to make sure his seat was right and sat down next to her. Within seconds she felt him stiffen as he caught the scent of her clothes, and she watched him from the corner of her eye as he attempted to covertly smell his underarms. It only took a cursory glance to see how visibly unkempt she was, and the man quickly realized it was her to blame for his singed nostril hair. Not wanting to be rude, he buried his face into his fist as nonchalantly as possible and remained that way until he disembarked at the next stop.

Seconds after the bus door swung shut behind him, the illuminated display at the head of the bus changed, and a sequence of three musical notes rang over the speakers.

"Next stop: 0xx-M-," said a woman's voice.

M looked around her. Everyone but her had filed off the bus already. Her stomach dropped and she wondered if she had made the wrong choice of destination. She considered calling out to the driver to let her off the bus when it jumped and began pulling away from the station.

Fuck it, she thought, and closed her eyes.

· · · ·

The bus pulled into 0xx-M- at 2:49am. The station had a single streetlamp on the platform, illuminating very little beyond the small station building, which was closed for the night.

The wooden boards of the platform protested beneath her feet as she stepped off the bus. She thanked the driver, and watched his taillights fade into the night.

Across the street was a motel and a gas station attached to a small convenience store. The motel had a large, backlit sign out front that cast an eerie red glow over the parking lot, which only had one car parked in it, a station wagon, presumably belonging to whoever was working that night. Below the large sign was a smaller neon one that read, perhaps redundantly, "VACANCY." She couldn't see much beyond that, as thick, dark, trees lined the horizon behind both buildings. The air was chilly, and the only sounds M could hear were the buzzing of the motel sign and her own breathing.

She grabbed her black duffel bag and tossed it over her shoulder before making her way across the street.

M pulled open the front door, knocking the bell above the doorway. The small, elderly woman sitting behind the desk gave out a short, high-pitched "whoo!" in surprise, almost dropping the paperback in her lap.

Regaining her composure, she greeted the stranger.

"Hello, dear! How can we help you?"

"I'm looking for a room. Do you do long-term rentals?" asked M.

The elderly woman stared blankly at her for a moment, as if M had been speaking another language. She muttered "long-term rentals" under her breath, and M could almost see her turning the phrase around her brain like a roast on a spit, until finally something clicked. You could almost hear it.

"Oh! Of course, dear. We can set that up for you, yes!"

M wondered if someone else was around. Nothing so far had led her to believe otherwise.

"How long might you be staying with us, darling?"

"I'm not sure. Do you need to know that to make the booking?"

"No, dear. We just like to make small talk. Pardon us if we've invaded your privacy."

"That's alright," replied M.

She filled out some paperwork and the elderly woman photocopied her driver's license and credit card for the room charges. She handed M the room key and informed her that breakfast would be served every morning at 6am. M thanked her and said that wouldn't be necessary. She was clearly the only guest, and there was no way she was waking up that early to eat alone with this woman.

She left the office and walked over to her room, number six. She paused at the door before looking towards the gas station. She hadn't eaten since that morning, and she felt it. Forgetting about the room for a moment, she dropped her bag at the door and made for the convenience store.

The gas station attendant wasn't quite as jumpy as the old woman from the motel. When M opened the door and the electronic bell chirped, he didn't so much as look up from his crossword, let alone yelp, so M looked around for something to eat.

She grabbed a few packs of ramen noodles and a small bag of salted pretzels. It wasn't ideal, but it would get the job done. She would find a real meal in the morning.

She put the items on the counter, and the attendant made the most god-awful noise as he hoisted his massive frame from the barstool in the corner. A cross between a grunt and a wheeze, the sheer amount of effort it seemed to take made M certain she was about to watch this man shit himself, if he hadn't already.

By the time he reached the register M could see beads of sweat on his brow. Without saying a word, eyes staring vacantly at the screen populating M's order, he scanned the food and gestured to the debit machine in between them. Behind his head, M noticed a row of liquor bottles and asked if he could add whatever one was cheapest to her bill.

He grunted something that sounded like "that'd be Jimmy," and grabbed a fifth of Jim Beam off the ledge. Concerned she was spending all her money on liquor; she asked if he might have a mickey instead. He chuckled, a sound not unlike gravel in a blender, and fell into a coughing fit.

"This ain't a liquor store, lady," he managed to get out.

"Fuck off," she replied, but said she would take it anyway. It had been a long day, and she knew that if she had to deal with Pizza The Hut any longer she might end up needing a second bottle.

The blender started up again, this time without the coughing fit, and the attendant pointed to the debit machine.

"Just pay for it and fuck off yourself. You smell like ass," he said.

The machine beeped at her to remove her card. M grabbed her items, but not before flipping him off. She heard the blender again as she stormed out the door.

· · · ·

The room was exactly what one would expect from a cheap, small-town motel across the street from a bus station. Beige walls, emerald green carpeting with disconcerting dark spots, a plain, stained wood desk with an electric kettle and coffee maker on it, a mini fridge that clearly used to be white but was now a sickly yellow, a large chipped wooden armoire with a small TV and satellite box, a telephone, lamp, and clock radio on the table next to the queen bed, and a bathroom that, had M not smelled worse herself, she would have bet reeked of mold. The lighting was dim and yellow, and every so often the ancient fluorescent bulbs behind the frosted ceiling panels would flicker loudly, temporarily turning the room into the saddest nightclub M had ever seen.

She dropped her duffel bag on the floor and grabbed the kettle for the ramen. As if on cue, her stomach protested. She pulled open the bag of noodles and pulled out the silver packet of soup mix before realizing she didn't have a bowl (or a spoon for that matter). She looked over at the coffee maker, and noticed a small mug tucked behind it. Bingo.

She crumbled the dry noodles into the mug, adding the soup mix and water once it had boiled. Immediately, scalding water began pouring through a crack in the handle, and M cursed as it ran down her wrist and onto the carpet. She dropped the mug and it cracked in two. She clutched her burned hand with the other and bolted for the bathroom, yanking open the tap in a frenzy and sticking her now bright red hand under the stream of cool water. It stung like a bitch. She tilted her head back to stifle the tears welling up in her eyes and took a deep breath. Then another. Then another.

When she had collected herself, she summoned the courage to look at her hand. Already blistering in a straight line from her thumb to her wrist, the rest of it seemed to emanate its own light, not unlike that of the motel sign in the parking lot out front.

She grabbed the hand towel from the bathroom counter and wrapped it up. Her stomach whined.

"I know, I know. I fucking know."

Looking over at the pile of half-soaked noodles and soup mix on the carpet, M couldn't help but let out a small whine herself. She took another deep breath, and decided to return her focus to food. She saw the pretzels sticking out of her bag on the floor and realized they were dinner.

She started into the bag, shoveling food into her mouth as fast as she could with her good hand. When she finished, she reached for the bottle of Jim Beam, poured herself a stiff drink using the glass from the bathroom, and slid onto the even stiffer motel bed.

CHAPTER FOUR

M woke up with a splitting headache.

Still in bed, fully clothed, she tried opening her eyes, bit by bit. The sun was already high in the sky, and the light made her head pound even worse. She went to close the curtain but used the wrong hand to prop herself up and let out a gasp as pain shot from the nerves in her burned hand straight to her throbbing skull, sending fireworks across her vision.

She rolled over to use her other hand and the empty bottle of Jim Beam fell to the floor with a dull *ka-klunk*. She kicked it out of the way and, eyes still mostly shut, felt her way across the room to the window. She yanked the curtain closed, and slowly opened her eyes the rest of the way.

As she took in her surroundings, the memory of the night before started creeping back into her mind, entirely in reverse, and with a few blank spots. She saw herself lying in bed with the bottle in hand, flipping aimlessly through TV channels. She saw her bright red, blistered hand. She saw the boiling water pouring down her wrist and onto the green carpet. She saw the gas station attendant, the old woman, the businessman on the bus. She saw the Chevelle.

"Nineteen-seventy-one Chevelle SS, all black with chrome detailing, leather interior, and one hell of an engine."

M laughed, and so did he. They both knew he didn't know shit about the engine. But this was the car that she and vV had drooled over since they had met, and here it was sitting in their driveway.

"Little bit cliché to buy a classic car with your advance, isn't it?" chided M.

vV shot her a look, holding back laughter.

"Fuck off."

They paused for a moment before vV spread his arms wide.

"Well? You wanna go for a ride or what?"

They both jumped in and tore off down the street. vV pulled onto the highway and let it rip. The engine roared, and M felt her chest pull back into the seat. Her heart raced. She looked over at vV's face, half glee, half focus, and swooned.

Gross, *she thought happily.*

M wiped the tears from her eyes and took a step towards the bathroom. Nausea flooded her senses, and she steadied herself on the nearest wall. She breathed deeply until it passed, then took another step. She repeated this process until she found herself in the doorway; sweat beading on her forehead. Rather than look in the mirror, she went straight for the shower. She crawled in and turned the water on.

Still clothed from the night before (and the night before that, and the night before that...), M let the water run all over her until she could feel the weight of soaked cotton weighing her down. She succumbed to that weight and sat on the shower floor. Piece by piece, and as slowly as she could without losing her lunch, M removed her sopping wet clothing until she was naked.

She looked to her immediate left and saw a small bottle of complimentary shampoo and body wash. She coached herself through the entire process, step-by-agonizing-step, until she was clean. By then the nausea had subsided slightly, and while her head still threatened to explode at the slightest provocation, she was grateful for that much.

She toweled off, rewrapped her hand in toilet paper, and threw on the only other set of clothes she had – black ripped jeans, a white t-shirt, and her leather jacket. She looked down at the empty bottle of Jim Beam still on the floor and cursed herself for finishing it. She really could have used something to take the edge off right about then. Maybe she'd grab another bottle while she was out. Just a mickey this time, though.

She left her room and went to the lobby. Opening the door slowly so as not to startle the old woman again, M entered and asked for directions into town.

"You missed breakfast, dear!" responded the elderly receptionist.

"Had a long night," croaked M.

"Well, that's quite alright. We hope you enjoyed your stay nonetheless."

M asked again about how to get into town, and this time was successful. She got change for the bus using a ten she had found in her jacket pocket and caught one in the direction she'd been instructed.

M marveled at how the daytime seemed to change her once sinister surroundings. All around the gas station and motel was a forested area that, the previous night, had seemed to stretch on forever into the abyss. After being on the bus for less than a minute, M saw it only went a couple hundred meters before opening back up to a rather bustling main road.

The first place to catch her eye was the diner. With a big cartoonish sign over the door reading "~~mon~~," M bee-lined in its direction. She knew there wasn't much room in her budget for eating out, and she would inevitably have to buy some proper groceries, but right now her stomach was screaming for real food, and she fully intended to accommodate it.

Styled after the 1950s, the diner looked about as kitschy as they come. When the waiter appeared in a white dress with red pinstripes and cap to match, M half-expected her to speak with a smoker's cough and end all her sentences with "hun." Thankfully, that wasn't the case.

"What can I get for ya?" she chimed.

"I'll have the hungryman combo."

M watched as the woman's eyes widened, just for a second, before looking her up and down, asking where she planned to put it all. Without breaking eye contact, M lifted her shirt just high enough to give her bare belly a hearty slap.

The waiter, reading her mood correctly, nodded and scurried off to the kitchen.

• • • •

Refueled, M decided to take a walk around town. Besides familiarizing herself with her new home for the next while, she needed a job and wasn't sure how else she was going to find one.

After an hour or so with no luck, she came across a grocery store. She pulled out her phone and opened her banking app. As the app loaded, her screen went black, and M remembered she had forgotten to charge it the night before.

Her head pounded as if to discipline her, and the nausea returned, though luckily not as bad as before. She leaned against a signpost to collect herself.

While she had been able to get down the entire hungryman meal, it had been an arduous process. One she didn't expect to be able to do again that day. Maybe, she bargained with herself, she'd just get something light to get her through the rest of the day and come back the following morning to do the rest of her shopping. That sounded reasonable.

Feeling slightly less like she was going to let loose a flurry of half-digested eggs and bacon, M steeled herself and entered ~~mins~~.

· · · ·

She ended up grabbing another bag of pretzels, jumbo size this time. The thought of putting anything more than bread in her stomach felt dangerous. Besides, she still had no way of cooking her own food anyway.

In the liquor aisle, she quickly found the mickey of Jim Beam and tossed it in her basket. It looked awfully small next to the pretzels. She pursed her lips and looked back at the shelf. A big yellow tag above the 750ml bottles read: buy 3 or more $19.95 each, less than 3 $27.49 each.

She turned the numbers over in her head for a while, before deciding three bottles was the way to go. Spending sixty dollars on booze was going to hurt, but if she could ration them properly she would end up saving quite a bit in the long run.

If nothing else, the discount makes up for the cost of breakfast, she reasoned.

She replaced the mickey with three fifths and promised herself she would reassess her budget when she got back to the motel room.

She passed the produce section on her way to the cash. A cardboard display showed a cartoon pirate with a speech bubble that read "The 9(a Department of Health recommends everyone eat 2-5 servings of fruit a day!" He was holding a comically large lemon, and M decided to take his advice, grabbing the yellow fruit from the display next to him. At the very least it'd go well with the whiskey.

Standing in line for the register, M watched her cashier apathetically slide each customer's items across the scanner, repeating a script he had committed so fully to memory she would have bet he didn't know what it meant anymore.

"Hello, welcome to ~~mins~~... will you be needing bags today... cash or credit... go right ahead... have a nice day... hello, welcome to ~~mins~~..."

When it was her turn, she watched him repeat his process, head down.

He was young, no more than thirty, and had longish, disheveled dark hair that tickled the tops of his ears. He had very prominent facial features that seemed to change the entire look of his face depending on the angle from which she viewed him.

When he reached the last item in her order (the lemon) he stopped, stared at it for a moment, laughed to himself, and said, "the breakfast of champions."

She laughed.

"Oatmeal's for suckers."

Years ago, she had read somewhere that good conversation should be like combat, and she was undefeated. She spoke like a boxer, ducking and dodging, delivering left hooks, right hooks, and uppercuts whenever she found an opening; most of the time leaving her opponent sprawled out on the mat before the end of the first round.

She made up a story about working at a bar she had noticed on her walk around town.

"So you're new to town?" he asked, passing her the receipt for her signature.

M thought about her answer. She wanted to say no, she was just passing through and would be gone within the month, but it only took one look at her order to make her think twice. Then it hit her that he might be flirting with her, and she decided to allow herself a little fun.

"Yeah," she replied, "see you 'round then, huh?"

She winked for good measure, grabbed her loot, and left.

$$\bullet\ \bullet\ \bullet\ \bullet$$

When she returned to the motel, M plugged in her phone and made herself a drink with the lemon, marveling at how quickly her headache faded into nothing. Sighing with relief, she sat upright in the bed and turned on the TV.

One drink turned into two, and two into three. Before she knew it the sun was down and she was drunk again. Her right hand pulsed underneath her bandage, and she thought to wash it.

When she returned to bed her stomach rumbled. She looked at the clock. 10:40pm. She grabbed the bag of pretzels and scarfed down half of it before making herself another drink.

Sick of the TV, she reached over to the clock radio and turned it on, hoping some background music might distract her from the heartbeat in her hand.

Throw your knife in the river
If it don't cut the way you know it should

You can't stand the modern lingo
The way that you could

M stared off at nothing, her whole body shaking. Her drink rattled over the edge of her glass and onto the bed sheets, but she made no move to do anything about it.

Your claim to fame is your lack of interest
And it's treated you well so far
She left a note on the kitchen table

M grabbed the clock radio, knocking over and spilling what was left of her drink, and threw it as hard as she could against the far wall. It made a loud crash, but clattered mostly unscathed, save for a nasty scratch across the top, straight down to the floor.

The sound shocked M out of her rage, and she burst into tears, sobbing loudly. She stayed that way for a good while, long after her stomach began cramping.

"Fuck you for getting off so easy," she said.

She grabbed the bottle of Jim Beam and took a swig. Her stomach finally got the better of her and she sprinted for the toilet.

CHAPTER FIVE

M woke up in the dark.

She inhaled a short, sharp breath, bracing herself for that familiar jolt of pain behind her eyes, and let it out slowly when it never came. Learning from previous mistakes, she rolled over and propped herself up on her good hand. She expected to find herself on the bathroom floor, so she was rather surprised to not only be in bed, but undressed as well.

She sat up on the edge of the bed and grabbed her phone to check the time. 5:42am.

Just in time for breakfast, she thought darkly.

She had a few missed calls as well. She swiped away the notifications and put her phone back on the bedside table.

She stood to make her way for the bathroom and lost her balance, scuffing her knees on the carpet on the way down. Her head swam, and M realized she was still drunk. That explained the lack of headache, and why she was on the floor.

She pulled herself up and turned on the bathroom light, shielding her eyes from the sudden change in brightness. As her vision adjusted, M used her good hand to feel her way to the toilet. She lifted the lid, pulled down her underwear, and sat down.

As she peed, she inspected her angry, pink knees. She hadn't broken the skin, luckily, but it seemed she was making a habit of hurting herself, and it wasn't a habit she was too keen on nurturing.

Finished, she wiped and returned to the living room, leaving the light on in the bathroom to avoid further injury while she reached for the bedside lamp. She dressed herself in the same clothes as the day before and made a mental note to find a laundromat while she was out.

She picked up the clock radio still on the floor and plugged it back in, resetting the time to match her phone. She ran her finger over the scratch she had made the night before and remembered the sound of its hard plastic casing hitting the wall.

Putting the thought out of her mind, M pulled on her boots and jacket and walked into the early morning.

The sun was starting to rise, barely peeking over the horizon. The air was crisp and filled with birdsong. She took a deep breath and exhaled loudly. Across the street, behind the platform where she had arrived the night before, a mother deer and its baby looked up in her direction briefly before disappearing into the woods behind them.

When she stepped into the lobby, M heard the receptionist before she saw her.

"Helloooo," sang the woman, "how lovely of you to join us for breakfast, dear!"

M nodded, briefly reconsidering her decision to get out of bed. She followed the receptionist into a small dining area.

The farthest wall from the entrance was lined with silver trays of bright yellow scrambled eggs, home fries, mini sausage links, bacon strips, two full loaves of bread (one white, one whole wheat), a toaster next to a tower of peanut butter, strawberry jam, and marmalade single-use packets, four open boxes of Kellogg's cereals, a coffee maker, a stack of mugs, plates, and bowls of various sizes, two jugs labeled "milk" and "cream," and a partitioned box of cloudy cutlery. M couldn't help but think this was a wildly inappropriate amount of food for one guest and did a quick three-sixty to make sure there wasn't anybody else there. There wasn't.

"Here you are, dear. Breakfast is nice! And! Warm!"

She punctuated each word with the wag of a finger.

"You can find the plates just over here, darling. And over here we have—"

"That's very kind of you, thanks," interrupted M, "I've got it."

The receptionist nodded before retreating to her desk. M sighed, relieved they wouldn't be sitting together, and began loading up her plate.

· · · ·

After breakfast, M hopped on a bus and made a quick trip to ~~mins~~ to grab some groceries. She was starting to sober up now and felt a headache coming on.

Inside, she loaded up her basket with items she wouldn't need to cook. She grabbed as many fruits and vegetables as she could carry, a loaf of bread, two packs of cold cuts, two jars of hummus, another jumbo bag of pretzels, and three boxes of granola bars.

She looked at her cart, unsatisfied. What she would have done for a microwave. She considered for a moment that she might be able to buy one there, but quickly tossed the idea out the window. Even a cheap microwave would set her back considerably, which reminded her she still needed to take that look at her credit balance.

Suddenly it dawned on her that her breakfast had to have been cooked somewhere in the motel, and it wasn't a stretch of the imagination that long-term guests might be entitled to kitchen privileges. M logged this useful piece of information and decided to look into it when she got back. Until then, she had enough to last her a few days, and that was a start. Besides, her headache was starting to reach a point where all she wanted was to get the hell out of there anyway.

"Excuse me, is your name M by any chance?" came a voice from her right.

Squinting against the harsh supermarket lighting, M looked over and saw a short, bearded, young man in his early twenties. He had long black hair tied up in a bun, and was wearing a buttoned-up red flannel and blue jeans. On his feet were the cleanest pair of white Converse M had ever seen, and she smirked at the way his whole body seemed to get dirtier the farther it got from the ground. She imagined him as a human root vegetable, just recently plucked from the earth by his immaculate Chucks and placed before her.

She didn't say anything, but rather stood motionless, squinting at him. He shuffled awkwardly back and forth, his soles squeaking comically on the linoleum.

"I'm sorry to bother you. I'm just... well, I'm a long-time listener and..." he trailed off self-consciously.

Not long ago, M had been a radio DJ in 7*t*hx* on a show highlighting the local music scene. Her dad had been a disc jockey in his day too, and, being a single dad, had often brought her into the studio with him throughout her childhood, cementing her love of music. When she was sixteen, she had asked her dad if she could get a job as an intern at the station, and through the miracle of nepotism she made it in and never left, working her way onto the team, and bouncing around positions for years until she finally got her own show. That was where she had met...

"Sorry, you must be confusing me with someone else," she said, and grabbed her cart to leave.

The inverted vegetable man stumbled over his words, and M was able to make out something about her being a dead ringer.

"She sounds hot. I've gotta get going, man."

He took the hint and, still tripping over his own self-consciousness, mumbled his way out of her life. She made for the cash registers, paid for her order, and left as fast as she could.

In the parking lot, a silver Elantra slowed at the crosswalk as she approached, and she recognized her cashier from the day before behind the wheel. Remembering how she had play-flirted with him, she winked. He winked back and she laughed.

Touché, she thought.

• • • •

Back in the motel room, M snapped open a newspaper someone had left behind at the bus stop and flipped straight to the classifieds. She sifted through tens of ads for dog-walkers and babysitters before she found a position with a remotely livable wage: receptionist at a car dealership.

She looked up at her reflection in the blank screen of the TV and laughed. She had a hard time imagining she had the look a small-town dealership was going for, but decided to give them a call nonetheless. A deep male voice answered.

"~~peat~~. jJj speaking."

"Hi there, I'm calling about the receptionist position. Can I speak with your manager?"

"Yeah, that's me. Come by the dealership this time tomorrow."

"For an interview?" asked M," of course, I'll be there."

"No, for a car," said jJj sarcastically. He chuckled, pleased with himself, before continuing.

"Yeah. For an interview."

M bit her tongue, reminding herself to prioritize her goal of gainful employment over her love of conversational combat, and left him her name and number before hanging up.

Well, she thought, *that's a start.* She took note of the time: 2pm.

She emptied her voicemail inbox in case anyone from ~~peat~~ tried to contact her. She didn't bother listening to any of her messages, and, instead, crossed the room to pour herself a drink, toasting her day's successes. She had gotten off to a rough start, but it seemed she might make it after all.

At the thought of "make it," she remembered she still hadn't checked her credit balance. She looked back across the room where her phone lay. It would only take a minute to do, but the thought of potentially ruining the first good day she had had since...

She decided that would be tomorrow's problem. She had only been in town two nights so far and surely couldn't have done *that* much damage in that time.

Sitting back down in bed, something caught M's eye. The newspaper lay spread out beside her and sticking off the edge of one of the pages was a picture of the headlight on a car.

Not just any car though, thought M, *a Chevelle.* And not just any Chevelle, a—

"*Nineteen-seventy-one Chevelle SS, all black with chrome detailing, leather interior, and one* hell *of an engine.*"

M grabbed at the page and pulled it out. The top corner read "lifestyle," and M saw it was a promotion piece about c&*, the band she had heard on the radio the night before. Four skinny, white men dressed all in different variations of black-on-black stood scowling in front of the car. Below it, the headline read: 7*t*hx* Locals c&* Bounce Back With New Single 'Modern Lingo.'

Reading no further, M balled up the page and threw it at the trashcan by the desk.

"Leave me the fuck ALONE," she said to the empty room.

She took a deep breath and grabbed the bottle of Jim Beam in place of her glass next to it.

CHAPTER SIX

Xxxxxx stared at the blank page in front of him. Its limitlessness fascinated him. Using the pen to his right, he could write a poem, a book, a letter. He could draw a map. He could create a whole new world, a new language, a new religion. He could fold up the paper into a swan, or an airplane. He could watch his words cut through the air like paper scissors through invisible ribbons, and he could watch them come crashing down under the weight of their own significance.

"Could," he said out loud, and wrote it on the page.

It was a silly word. It seemed to carry around more letters than it needed, and Xxxxxx wondered if the extra letters were some ancient linguist's joke, a visual representation of all the potential the word carried.

"Could, could, could."

He chewed on the word, turning it over and over in his head, looking at it from all angles until, much like with real chewing, he found the word had turned to mush. It no longer resembled itself, and as such Xxxxxx couldn't quite remember what it meant anymore.

He put the pen down and looked over at a smaller piece of paper to the left of the one he was just writing on. It was the paper with M's number on it. He picked it up and spun it around in his fingers a few times.

Xxxxxx was aware of society's peculiar texting policies but had never understood them. He had watched sitcom after sitcom of friends berating each other for coming across as needy if you texted someone too soon after meeting them, or too aloof if you texted them too late, and while it meant absolutely nothing to him, Xxxxxxx knew better than to assume that of others. So, he did his best to play by the rules.

What would he say anyway? Hi, I'm Xxxxxxx and I want to be your friend? Would you like to play on the swings with me?

"Could," he said again, and laughed.

He settled on inputting her number into his phone so he wouldn't lose it and left it at that. He balled up the page in front of him and put it in the bottom drawer of his desk before walking back into the living room. He turned on the TV manually, grabbing a mason jar of weed on the way to his recliner.

As he rolled himself a joint, a line from the song he had heard the night before popped into his head.

You can't stand the modern lingo
The way that you could

There was that word again. The way that you *could.* Xxxxxxx licked the sticky side of the rolling paper as he considered what the line meant. He had initially understood it as a rejection of youth culture, maybe coming from the perspective of someone older, but now he wasn't so sure. That word "could," changed the feeling of the whole line. It was clear that whoever it was the singer was talking to was someone capable of fitting in but was making a choice not to. Xxxxxxx tried to remember more of the song so he could dive further into his theory, but couldn't recall the melody anymore, let alone more lyrics.

He sparked up his joint and inhaled deeply. He wondered what M might be doing at that moment. He imagined her behind the bar at ~~une~~, pouring a pint while she took the next patron's order. He imagined himself being that patron, ordering an Old Fashioned, and discussing the endless possibilities of "could" with her as she worked.

Too high now to drive, Xxxxxx resolved to make a trip down to ~~une~~ the following night. If nothing else, it would beat sitting at home pretending to write.

CHAPTER SEVEN

There was a knock on the door.

"Housekeeping!" sang the motel receptionist.

M's mouth smacked loudly as she peeled it open to say she was coming, but her lip split before any sound could come out. She gasped in pain, instinctively raising her hand to her face only to find she couldn't feel anything past her left shoulder.

She opened her eyes. She was on the floor next to her bed, her left arm stuck underneath her body, asleep. She used her bandaged hand to push herself onto her back, cursing under her breath the whole way. Moments later, she felt pins and needles as feeling began to creep back into her lifeless arm.

Satisfied with the lack of reply, the elderly receptionist pushed open the front door to the room only to be stopped by the chain lock. She let out a small "ooh!" and quickly pulled the door shut, apologizing profusely from the other side until her voice faded into the distance. M let out a small sigh of relief. At least that was one less thing she had to deal with.

By now all the feeling had returned to her arm, and she was able to lift herself off the floor and onto the bed. She moved slowly, receiving a sharp stab in the temples every time she tried to quicken her pace.

She grabbed her phone from the nightstand and turned it on. The screen came to life, illuminating a vast network of cracks all over the front of the device.

Fuck me, she thought, *not you, too.*

She was still in the same clothes she had been wearing since her first night in 0xx-M-, so she stuffed the phone into the back pocket of her jeans before remembering she had forgotten to check it in the first place. She pulled it out again and saw, in addition to the calls she'd grown accustomed to, three missed calls and one voicemail from the same unknown number. She cursed, remembering her interview at the dealership, when she saw it was only noon. She still had a couple hours left to wash some clothes before heading into town. Some breakfast wouldn't hurt either.

Significantly less panicked, she opened her voicemail and turned on the speakerphone. The same deep voice from the dealership boomed from the internal speaker.

"This is jJj from ~~peat~~. I don't know if this is supposed to be some kind of sick joke or somethin', but if you were feeling lucky about that receptionist position you can forget about it. Can't even answer your *own* fucking phone..."

The message clicked loudly as he hung up. Confused, M checked when the message was sent. 8:37am. What could she have done overnight that he wouldn't even interview her anymore?

She checked the times on the other two missed calls. The most recent was 2:45pm, and the first one 2:20pm.

That's weird, she thought. How had she missed two calls 45 minutes after placing the first one? She double-checked her phone wasn't set to silent, and found that not only was the volume on, but maxed out as well.

Her head screamed at her, making it difficult to focus. Her vision was blurry, and she was just about to give up trying to decipher the numbers dancing on the screen in front of her when she saw it. Right at the top, next to the 8:37am call, was the date: Monday, June 5th. M's interview was for 2pm on the 4th. Somehow, she had lost an entire day.

As if on cue, she doubled over and vomited onto the carpet beside her bed. She tried for the bathroom and her migraine sliced through her skull, only causing her to vomit more. So she sat there, head between her legs, until it passed. She let out a single sob when it was over and wept into her hands.

· · · ·

After she cleaned up, she forced down a dry piece of bread and took a shower, washing her clothes at the same time. She tried to piece together as much of the last couple days as she could.

She remembered coming home from the store. She remembered setting up the interview. She remembered feeling hopeful. She remembered pouring a drink to celebrate her successes. After that it started getting fuzzy. She saw flashes of imagery like an overexposed slideshow, all so out of focus she couldn't make sense of any of it.

She began to ask herself how she had allowed the drinking to get so bad so fast before putting the thought out of her mind. She knew why. It was why she was in this town. It was why she had taken the bus when there was a perfectly good car sitting in the driveway. It was why she hadn't washed her clothes in a week.

She got out of the shower and toweled off, hanging her clothes to dry on the curtain rod. Her hangover had abated slightly, and the feeling of being clean left M feeling significantly more optimistic about the day ahead.

That optimism dwindled slightly when she saw the state of her food supply. Save for a few slices of bread and a moldy bag of oranges, she was out. She would have to make a trip to the store before the end of the day.

Her booze was also gone, but that was no surprise.

When enough of her clothes had dried that she could put together a full outfit, M got dressed and made her way into town. The sun had already set, so ~~mins~~ was mostly empty by the time she got there, save for one or two other customers.

Since she had neglected to ask about using the motel kitchen, she grabbed many of the same items as her previous trip, including the three bottles of Jim Beam. The whiskey was still on sale, but she knew she could no longer fool herself into thinking that was the reason she was buying so many. Not anymore.

She placed the bottles gingerly into her cart with a feeling of relief. There was something almost freeing about it. She wasn't proud of her drinking, to put it lightly, but at least now she didn't feel the need to justify her obvious lack of self-control. It felt as if she'd been hiding it behind a curtain of rationalization since she'd arrived in 0xx-M-, and finally the curtain had been pulled away. All that was left to decide was if that meant the show was starting or had just finished.

As she approached the cash, she looked for her new favourite cashier. She saw him at the end of the line and made her way to him. Another cashier called out to her on the way down, an older woman who looked like she slept in a jar of formaldehyde, and M made as if to change her mind before veering off at the last second back to her intended lane. The woman sucked her teeth loudly in disappointment, and M had to bite her lip to keep her composure.

Not missing a single thing, the male cashier burst out laughing.

"Howdy, stranger," said M.

"Stocking up for another round I see," he said, as she placed the whiskey onto the belt. His word choice amused M, and she donned her boxing gloves.

"You bet. Cage match, anything goes!"

He wobbled but didn't go down.

"In this corner, wearing the white trunks, we've got Jimmy the Beam, weighing two-point-two-five litres—"

M parried his attack and countered with her own. She saw a spark light behind his eyes, and they entered a blow-for-blow showdown, playing out the rest of the bit. It had been a while since M had faced a worthy opponent, and she reveled in it. It could be lonely being king.

Finally, she saw an opening and took it. The cashier doubled over in laughter, and she hoisted the championship belt triumphantly over her head. The win secured, she laughed as well.

"Not much for entertainment 'round here, is there?" she asked.

"Not really," he agreed.

"Well, aren't I glad I found you then, huh?"

He blushed, and M got in one last jab before wrapping up her order and heading back to the motel.

She got off the bus a stop early. The one she usually got off at put her right within view of the motel's front office, and after that morning the last thing she wanted was to run into the receptionist.

Once inside, she emptied her groceries, and poured herself a drink as she looked over that day's classifieds. It didn't look any different than the day before, so M tossed the paper in the trash and started on a sandwich for dinner.

It had dawned on her on the way home that she might benefit from getting into a routine. Maybe if she structured her days, she would run less of a risk of having them blur all together. Maybe she would be able to remember all the little things she kept forgetting to do. Maybe it would keep her from drinking as much. Maybe.

There certainly wasn't any harm in trying, anyway.

• • • •

It took about a week before M felt herself falling into a rhythm, but it was a welcome feeling when it did arrive. She set her phone's alarm to go off at 6am every morning so she could eat a free breakfast, then she would return to the room, shower, and head into town to look for work. Her hand had almost entirely healed, and she no longer needed the bandage.

She still hadn't found a steady job but picked up a few dog-walking gigs for a little extra cash. She would return to the motel for lunch, then head back out until the sun went down. Most of the time she would find herself kicking stones down the road, but she knew staying out of the motel meant she wouldn't drink, so she chose the lesser of two evils.

She still drank at least a fifth of whiskey a night, and a little in the morning to help with the hangover. Her routine kept her bingeing in check for a while, but over time her morning shot became a glass, and her evening drink became her mid-afternoon drink, and so on. Eventually she bought a flask, figuring she wouldn't need to worry about being hungover if she never stopped drinking in the first place.

One night, she realized in a panic that she hadn't had her period since she got to town. She was usually pretty good at predicting when it would start, within one or two days on either side, but that night she was overdue by almost a full week, an unprecedented amount of time. It made no sense that she would be pregnant, so M took to the internet to find a solution. A quick search determined it could be due to stress, poor diet, or heavy drinking. In her case it could have been any of those, maybe even all of them, so she put it out of her mind, deciding to count it as a win instead. No period meant no cramps, and no need to buy tampons, which meant more money for food. Or whiskey.

Every few days she would stop by ~~mins~~. She would pick up the same items and, as long as he was working, spar with her favourite cashier, whose name she eventually learned was Xxxxxxx. It had been on his nametag the whole time; she just hadn't cared to check before then.

Her play-flirting naturally dropped off with time and M began to view Xxxxxxx as something close to a friend. He was sharp, if a little in his own head, and she appreciated that. She didn't feel the need to pull punches when she spoke to him. So when he asked for her number she gave it to him without hesitation. She considered how nice it might be to have an ally; someone to help her find some work and get back on the road.

CHAPTER EIGHT

The debit machine beeped loudly. Xxxxxxx leaned over it to read the error message.

Declined. Insufficient funds.

"Huh. Here, try it again."

He tapped in a quick command on his till and reset the machine. M swiped her card again, and the machine made the same horrible noise.

Her heart sank. Suddenly she remembered all the times she had attempted to check her credit balance, and how every time she had either been interrupted or too lazy to do so. How the urgency had faded in her memory. How it had been replaced by pride. Pride for remembering to do laundry, or for following up on a job. They all flashed across her mind like some sadistic movie where she was the lead, and the plot was just how much she sucked.

"Fuck, I swore I paid this off," she covered.

"Do you have anything else you can use? A debit card, maybe? I'm sure your boss can just reimburse you."

She furrowed her brow as she tried to make sense of his last statement. Her boss? She remembered the lie she had made about working at ~~une~~ on her first visit, though the name of the bar escaped her.

She looked down at her groceries, now much more than booze, pretzels, and a lemon, and wondered how Xxxxxxx could possibly still think this was for a bar. She had noticed that while he had an ability to see the world from different and interesting perspectives, he also tended to miss the forest for the trees, as they say.

As far as her debit card was concerned, M had drained the last of her savings to afford the bus trip that had brought her there. Her credit card was totally paid off at the time, so she had planned to use it as a stopgap until she found work. She knew it was a bad idea, but at the time staying in 7*t*hx* had seemed like a worse one. Now here she was, three weeks in, broke.

Before she could come up with an excuse, Xxxxxxx spoke up.

"You know what? Don't worry about it. How about I get this one and you get me back another time?"

Without waiting for a reply, he pulled a black leather wallet out of his back pocket and produced his own credit card. He swiped it, signed the store's copy of the receipt as it printed, and passed the other over to M. She looked around for her boxing gloves and couldn't find them anywhere.

"I... thank you," she said.

"Don't mention it," smiled Xxxxxxx.

Rattled, M grabbed her groceries and walked out the door to the bus stop.

· · · ·

"FUCK!" M screamed into the empty motel room, slamming the door behind her. She grabbed the nearest empty bottle and hurled it across the room. It bounced off the corner of the bed and rolled harmlessly across the carpet, only making a small *tonk* as it bumped the leg of the desk.

Unsatisfied by the lack of destruction, M grabbed a full bottle from her bag, opened it, and threw her head back, pouring the whiskey down her throat.

Her phone pinged.

She dropped the arm holding the bottle to her side, and checked her message. It was from an unknown number.

Hey, it's Xxxxxxx. Just got my lunch break. Wanna grab a bite if you're still around?

She looked down at the bottle in her hand, then back at the phone as another text came in.

On me. ;)

She laughed, surprising herself.

Not wanting to pass up a free meal, M replied saying she could be at ~~mon~~ in ten. She capped the bottle and walked right back out the door.

• • • •

By the time M arrived, Xxxxxxx had already polished off his burger and was making good headway on his fries. He was seated in a booth by the front window and waved at her through the glass as she crossed the parking lot.

She sat across from him and waved down the waiter. The same woman that had served her breakfast so many days ago approached with a pad and pen.

"The hungrywoman returns!" she chided.

"Bring me your finest meats!" M said in her best impression of royalty. She banged her fist on the table jovially.

The waiter laughed.

"What can I get for ya?"

"I'll have what he's having," said M, nodding at Xxxxxxx's plate.

"One burger n' fries, comin' up!"

She checked in with Xxxxxxx and turned on her heels to pass the order off to the kitchen.

"So!" exclaimed M, breaking the ice, "Xxxxxxx. The man, the mystery. Tell me all about him. Does he live a real human life outside the grocery store?"

She wanted to control the conversation. She had learned from her radio days that most people relish the opportunity to talk about themselves when given the chance, so by keeping the ball in his court she wouldn't have to explain who she was and why she was in 0xx-M-.

X laughed.

"No ma'am. When the lights turn off he folds into the register to recharge overnight."

"Livin' rent free in a box full of money! You guys hiring?"

She wasn't entirely joking about that last part.

"Can you do this?" He moved his right hand back and forth horizontally, mimicking the motion of scanning items on a register.

"Jerk off your boss? If that's all it takes you'll be working for me by July."

Pow, right in the kisser. Xxxxxxx threw his head back, cackling, and M steered the conversation back on course.

"So is the capitalist-sex-toy life the life for you, or were you programmed for a higher calling?"

She caught him taking a sip of his water and he spit it back up into his glass at the phrase "capitalist-sex-toy."

"I'm not sure how I'm supposed to answer that."

"Try this: I ain't no capitalist sex doohickey! I'm a real boy! Or whatever. Make it your own."

He scratched the back of his neck, visibly uncomfortable.

"I dunno, I guess you could say I'm a writer."

"Why do I have to say it? What's stopping you?"

"Sounds pretentious, I guess."

"Fuck 'em."

Xxxxxxx smiled, and M continued her line of questioning.

"What do you write?"

"Mostly trash," he said.

A blow to the temple, and M saw stars. A sharp burst of laughter escaped from her lips.

"I write poetry," he continued, "Free verse. I don't like structured art much."

"Why's that?"

"Structure dictates direction. When I choose a word, it's because I want that word. I don't want to swap it out for another because it has too many syllables or doesn't rhyme with the line I wrote before it. I chose it because it means what I want to say. Structure tells you where you need to put your ideas. It's the colour-by-numbers of art."

"You're right, that does sound pretentious," said M.

Xxxxxxx blushed, and M winked at him.

"I'm only joking. You make a good point. When I want to call someone a cunt, I *only* want to call them a cunt. 'Meanie' just doesn't cut the way it should."

Throw your knife in the river, sang a voice in their heads.

"See, you get it!" laughed Xxxxxxx.

"Can I read any of your work anywhere?"

"Nah," he replied, playing with the fries on his plate.

The waiter returned with M's combo, and M enthusiastically asked her if she had read any of Xxxxxxx's poetry. The waiter gasped dramatically.

"Xxxxxxx! I didn't know you wrote poetry! You *must* read me some someday!" she chimed.

Xxxxxxx was a blubbering mess. He kept starting sentences and abandoning them halfway through, like Frogger jumping from car to car only to realize each one was as damning as the last.

Since he was covering lunch, M thought she'd help him out.

"Dang! He *just* did a reading last night too. Oh well, maybe if he ever decides to come back out of retirement..."

The waiter turned to M with a confused look on her face.

"Retirement," the waiter mirrored.

"Long and illustrious career, this one. Maybe you can make the award ceremony at city hall on Friday!"

By now the waiter picked up on the bit and laughed, a good sport. She made sure both Xxxxxxx and M had everything they needed and returned to the kitchen.

"So, I take it your writing is more of a private deal," said M, backpedalling slightly.

"Yeah," said Xxxxxxx, smirking.

"How come?"

"There's nothing great about it."

"Why does it have to be great?" challenged M.

"Because my art will outlive me. It's the only tool I have to tell the world who I am, independent of their own perceptions. It's the only way anyone will get it right, you know?"

M understood what he meant but wasn't sure she agreed. So instead of answering right away, she folded her arms and leaned back into her seat, pursing her lips while trying to turn her thoughts into words.

"Who you are isn't how you feel, though. It's all about who you know. The people around you decide what kind of person you are."

Xxxxxxx was taken aback.

"How does that make any sense? If I knew how to juggle but never told anyone, are you saying I wouldn't actually know how to juggle?"

M grasped desperately at the thought as it blurred in her mind. Her moment of clarity had very quickly frayed at the edges, and now she was left staring at the hazy outline of what she had meant. While she was very adept at quick, witty conversation, heavy conceptualizing had never been her bag.

"It's not that you wouldn't know how to juggle. It's more that no one would describe you as a juggler, I guess."

"I'm not sure I follow."

"Okay, okay, put it this way. Let's say some guy comes up to you and starts going off about how nice a person he is. Ten bucks says you think 'yeah, right. Whatever,' right?"

X nodded. He was squinting at M while he listened, as if he might be able to see her point if he just tried hard enough.

"Now imagine a different scenario where someone else comes up to you and points across the room at the first guy. He tells you that guy over there is the nicest dude he's ever met. Do you think you're going to be as skeptical?"

Now it was Xxxxxxx's turn to fold his arms and lean back into his seat. His brow furrowed and he looked down at the table, focusing on nothing. His head spun. It wasn't as if he was trying to come up with a counterargument, in fact he knew she was right, but the implications of what she said left him feeling utterly baseless. For years he had comforted himself with thoughts of societal retribution through his writing; that maybe others would see him for the bright mind he was if only he could tell them in his own words. But now he realized that it didn't matter if his inner thoughts made Shakespeare read like Munsch. It didn't matter if he heard symphonies in his head. He still spoke like a cashier and couldn't hum a tune if his life depended on it.

"Fuck," he said.

M knew from the way he strung those four letters together that she had gotten her point across. What she hadn't expected was the sullen silence that followed.

Right on cue, the waiter appeared with the check. M nodded in Xxxxxxx's direction and winked. The waiter winked back and placed the check on Xxxxxxx's end of the table before saying she would be back in a minute. Xxxxxxx pulled out a wad of bills from his uniform pocket and dropped them onto the table.

"I gotta get back to work," he said.

"Thanks for lunch!" said M enthusiastically.

She was starting to feel guilty for putting Xxxxxxx in such a funk when, without warning, his face changed. She couldn't put her finger on the specifics of what happened; only that he looked... reset. He smiled and offered to walk her to the bus stop. She declined and thanked him for the offer.

"Where is it you live, anyway?" he asked.

"You know that alleyway behind ~~peat~~?" she replied.

Xxxxxxx cackled, throwing his head back.

"Alright, alright. You keep your secrets."

M winked at him, and they walked out the front door together.

CHAPTER NINE

M returned to the motel to find a note slipped underneath the door to her room. It was from the motel claiming her credit card had bounced, and could she please visit the front desk at her earliest convenience?

She tossed the note in the trash and grabbed the bottle she had left behind less than an hour earlier before sitting on the edge of the bed. If this was going to be her last night here, she would need to come up with a new plan, and quick.

She wondered if Xxxxxxx would be understanding of her situation. All signs seemed to point to yes, but she felt a lump in her throat at the thought of telling him she had been lying to him this whole time; and just hours after he'd covered her ass *and* bought her lunch.

She washed the lump down with a glug of whiskey and crossed the room to her duffel bag. Still half-packed, if you could call what she'd done "packing", she threw it on the bed and began stumbling around the room, retrieving what little she'd removed from it three weeks ago.

Still irresolute about calling Xxxxxxx, M knew one thing for sure: she had to get out of the motel. Where she would go, she had no clue. That was something she could figure out tomorrow. The old woman would surely be by in the morning, and she didn't want to find out if the "we" she kept referring to was some kind of alter ego who only came out for the bad customers. M laughed a little at that, imagining her as an alien from a Men in Black rewrite before her neural pathways took the reference and ran with it, recalling the four black-clad, scowling twenty-somethings she'd seen in the newspaper earlier that month.

*c&**, she remembered. They were all almost comically serious, standing in front of that gorgeous black '71 Chevelle. All of them but one, anyway. Third from the left, he had had a smirk on his face that, if only because M already knew, betrayed who the car belonged to.

Her heart rate accelerated, and she threw her head back, pouring whiskey down her throat until she began choking on it. She turned spastically to grab a t-shirt she had left on the chair, tripped over herself, and watched the corner of the desk come up to meet her.

PART TWO

CHAPTER TEN

"You awake?"

No one replied.

"Ah, well."

vV couldn't sleep. His head swam pleasantly, buzzing gently atop his pillow.

He couldn't believe it. It had all paid off. He had fucking done it.

After nine years of grinding and grinding and grinding, c& had finally signed with a major label. Their last single had been a huge success, garnering well over one million plays within its first month on organic reach alone, and as a result the band had spent the last few weeks meeting with label exec after label exec trying to capitalize on the band's newfound notoriety. Each one dangled a bigger and nicer carrot than the one before it, until finally Brutal Baby Records reached out.*

Now, Brutal Baby wasn't necessarily one of the biggest players in the music industry, but vV and the guys had all grown up on their roster, and there was a certain value to that they couldn't overlook. vV remembered when the band first started, back in cCccc's garage, when they would all butcher Black Spoon covers and swap tapes of different Brutal Baby artists.

That was before Hh joined the band, *thought vV. He laughed, recalling how shrill they had sounded before finding a bassist.*

M stirred in her sleep beside him.

"Shit. Sorry," he whispered.

He was met with a loud snore in reply.

vV snapped back into his internal monologue. Here he was nine years later, the ink barely dry on his very own record deal with the label that had made him pick up a guitar so long ago. No shit he couldn't sleep.

He gingerly got out of bed and pulled on his underwear before creeping across the bedroom, avoiding the squeaky floorboards. He pulled the door shut behind him and started down the hallway, steadying himself against the wall. He and M had celebrated the signing together, just the two of them, over a bottle of Woodford Reserve, and he was still pretty bombed.

He made it into the foyer and began pulling on his shoes and a long coat when an inquisitive whine came from the corner of the room.

"It's just me, bud. Go back to bed."

The blue heeler lowered its head back onto its bed and let out a huff.

"Yeah yeah, I'll keep it down," said vV before walking out the front door of the house.

He crossed the front lawn and the motion detector above the shed's front door turned on the flood light. He paused for a second, just to look at the structure he'd been thinking of moments before – all natural wood, no markings or signage anywhere except for a stencil of the word "SHED" spray-painted in black on the front door, complete with a tiny black triangle roof above it.

Inside, the shed was furnished with two mismatched couches, an armchair, a small coffee table, a drum kit, a few stacks of amplifiers, a grandfather clock, a desk chair, and half a wall of recording equipment. Strewn over, under, across, between, and around just about everything in the room was a tangled web of black instrument and microphone cables.

vV sat in the armchair and snatched a piece of paper off the coffee table. It was the paperwork for a 1971 Chevelle, his dream car.

Three years before, after M had interviewed c& on 107.7fm, the two had bonded over a shared love of classic cars, despite knowing practically nothing about them. In particular, they had both expressed a love for the slightly less popular 1971 model of Chevelle. So, when news came in of the contract with Brutal Baby and the massive advance that was coming with it, vV had had the paperwork drawn up to be signed as soon as everything was finalized with the label. In other words, today.*

He stared at his signature on the page. He hadn't told M about the car yet, hoping to surprise her with it. She had been remarkably cool with the amount of time he had been spending away from home, whether it was these last few weeks bouncing in and out of the city for label meetings, or the lengthy tours in the months preceding that, and thought this surprise would be a good way to say thank you.

Plus, it was a sick *car.*

He tossed the contract back on the table and moved over to the desk chair. He pulled up to the reel-to-reel on the desk in front of him and flicked it on. He turned the lever, and the reels began to move. He sat back in the chair and listened.

Throw your knife in the river

If it don't cut the way you know it should

You can't stand the modern lingo

The way that you could

Your claim to fame is your lack of interest

And it's treated you well so far

She left a note on the k—

vV turned the lever back, his brow furrowed.

"Something weird still going on in the low mids," he said to no one, before jotting those same words down on a notepad next to him on the table.

Besides being their teenage heroes, one of the reasons c& had signed with Brutal Baby was that they would be able to keep producing their own recordings. vV had grown alongside the band as their unofficial recording engineer and had become quite good over the years. As his self-taught approach refined, his techniques gave the band a unique sonic characteristic that became baked in with their overall sound. They knew changing hands would change their entire aesthetic, so it became a non-negotiable part of their agreement that vV remain their man, and luckily for them Brutal Baby was happy to oblige.*

vV snuck back into the house and crawled into bed. He considered taking a hit from the bong in the living room to knock him out before remembering how drunk he still was and decided better of it.

Instead, he lay on his back and stared at the same tiny crack in the ceiling he'd been staring at just fifteen minutes ago.

Holy shit. He had fucking done it.

CHAPTER ELEVEN

Xxxxxx clocked out and made his way to the employee exit on the loading dock. He had spent the remainder of his shift drifting in and out of the present, constantly returning to his conversation with M at ~~mon~~.

"Who you are isn't how you feel, though. It's all about who you know."

He couldn't tell if he was more devastated at what felt like his whole worldview being upended, or ecstatic that he now felt had the answer he had been looking for. In fact, it made more sense to him the longer he thought about it. His entire career at ~~mins~~ had led his coworkers to believe he was a beacon of sunshine and, were he to die in his sleep that very night, that sentiment would be his legacy, regardless of its validity.

He remembered how their waiter had perked up when M mentioned his poetry, and a rather dark thought came to join an already lightless monologue. What if, by sheer nature of the small size and insular nature of 0xx-M-, the garbage he left in his bottom drawer was all he needed to get the recognition he craved so fiercely?

Having reached his car, Xxxxxx paused at the door and shook his head before unlocking it and crawling inside. He'd rather die a nobody than be loved for mediocre work, even if only mediocre by his standards.

He pulled onto the road, heading west.

After buying M lunch he worried that visiting her at work might be coming on a bit too strong. He had planned to bring it up at ~~mon~~, but obviously had had other things on his mind at the time.

He pulled into the ~~une~~ parking lot.

At one point a thriving strip mall, ~~une~~ now stood as the only storefront at the end of a long row of dilapidated, unoccupied units. The bar stood out like an overdressed pool boy at a country club, all bright and cheery, oblivious to its disappointed, greying onlookers.

Loud country music poured out the front door every time someone came or went, and Xxxxxxx felt his resolve waver in time with the lap steel. This wasn't his scene. Maybe he should just go home, grab a beer he'd already paid for, roll up a joint, and veg out on his recliner. That sounded really nice.

Just then RRr, the bar owner, popped out the side door for a smoke. Xxxxxxx saw his opportunity and pulled up beside him.

RRr, or Big R for short, had taken over ~~une~~ from his father, who had taken over for his father before that (keeping the locals liquored ran in the family). He was a big man, in every sense of the word. Standing at six feet three inches, and weighing almost three hundred pounds, he certainly wasn't the kind of guy who wasted his money on silly things like security staff. He wore a loose muscle shirt and was covered in faded tattoos that poked through the thick, dark hair all over his arms, shoulders, and back.

But as large as Big R was, his big, bushy moustache transformed him from prison inmate to cartoon strongman with the twitch of his nose.

"Hey RRr, how's it going?" said Xxxxxxx, leaning out the window.

"Hey! Uh..." RRr hesitated.

"Xxxxxx," said Xxxxxx.

"Xxxxxx! Big Xxxxxx! Sorry pal. Things are great. How 'bout you? Whatcha doin' out here? Thought you lived in the east end," prattled RRr.

"I do. I'm here to see uh... shit," cursed Xxxxxx.

Xxxxxx went bright red. Hearing himself say it out loud he realized how desperate he must look, leaving the depths of his dungeon for the fair maiden in the tower. His internal spiral was interrupted by Big R's hearty laugh, which practically rattled the frame of his car.

"Here to see shit, eh? Aren't we all!"

He burst into laughter again, and Xxxxxx glanced nervously in the direction of his car's airbag.

"Here to see M," Xxxxxx squeezed out.

"Who?"

"M."

"Just M? Ain't heard that before."

Impressed, RRr's mouth pulled downwards into his chin, and his moustache bristled.

"Yeah, just M," said Xxxxxx, a perplexed look on his face. He had lost track of the conversation.

They both stood staring at each other for a moment, before RRr broke the silence.

"So... who's M?" he asked.

Xxxxxx squinted and poked his face out towards RRr. Was this some kind of joke? He decided to play it straight until he was sure.

"Uh, your new bartender?"

Now it was RRr's turn to be confused. He jerked his head back and blinked a few times.

"I ain't got a new bartender, pal. You alright?"

Concern flashed behind his eyes, and Xxxxxx's stomach dropped. His brain, on the other hand, remained ignorant of his fumbling gut and continued trying to remind RRr who his newest staff member was.

"You know, reddish hair, curly, tattoos, piercings."

With each descriptor Xxxxxx waved his arms around the corresponding parts of his own body.

"I have no idea what you're talkin' about, Xxxxxx. I ain't never heard of no M, and I certainly ain't never hired one. Don't know what to tell ya," said Big R as he ashed his smoke. Xxxxxx could tell he was trying to break it to him easy. He never used the word "sorry," but passed the sentiment down through his soft, compassionate tone.

Xxxxxx, tail wedged firmly between his legs, apologized shyly and pulled back out of the parking lot, his mind reeling. Besides being one of the more embarrassing experiences in recent memory, he couldn't wrap his head around its implications. Everything he had built up in his mind about M was false. She had lied to him.

Why? he thought. He racked his brain for a reason but couldn't think of anything past M being a sadist, playing a cruel trick on the dumb, small-town cashier with no future.

He flew down the highway, going 145km/h. He was livid. How could he have been so *stupid*? He knew she seemed too good to be true. He cycled through every past interaction in his head, seeing each one now in an insidious new light. Every wink, every joke was now just a ploy to gain his trust. And he *had* trusted her. That's what made him so mad. He had never opened up to anyone in the way he had opened up to her.

She was his best friend, he realized, and wept the rest of the way home.

CHAPTER TWELVE

Hh nodded a thank you at vV for holding the door open for him. Everyone inside, vV let it close behind him and turned into the 107.7fm lobby.

To promote their latest single, Hh had secured an interview for c& on M's show using connections from a former group. The single wasn't doing as well as they had anticipated, and the band hoped the sheer volume of 107.7fm listeners would be enough to snag them a few new fans before the song played itself out.*

The lobby looked like a repurposed comic book store; decked out from floor to ceiling in the station's signature purple and green colour scheme. From doorknobs to electrical sockets to wainscotting to carpets, not a single detail hadn't been painstakingly selected or painted to match the motif.

vV moved over to the east wall and sat down on the shiny green couch against it. It made a rubbery squelch when he sat on it, and the hair raised on the back of his neck as a shiver ran down his spine. He shuddered. cCccc laughed at his reaction as he joined him on the couch, only to eat his words seconds later after experiencing the same sickening squelch.

"Dude. What the fuck," he said.

Both men burst into laughter, drawing disapproving looks from Hh and qQQQ, who were speaking with the receptionist at the front desk just feet away. They hushed up as well as they could as the others finished checking in and came back to meet them.

"Said she'll be out in a minute," said qQQQQ.

"Here, have a seat," said cCccc, gesturing to the empty cushion beside him.

qQQQ and Hh sat down and met their fate just as the first two had, only Hh let out a high-pitched "hoo!" at the unpleasant sensation, causing all four men to burst into a giggle fit.

To the left of the front desk, a bright green door swung open on purple hinges and a pair of black Doc Martens crossed the purple threshold. M took one look at the four bandmates clutching their bellies, tears streaming down their faces, and snapped her mouth shut as quickly as her jaw would allow.

Save it for the interview, she thought. It was a well-rehearsed method of hers to keep the gloves off until the red light was on. Give 'em what they've got coming when the cameras were rolling. She could practice on the interns; this was showtime.

At the sound of M's teeth clacking shut, the band looked up and quickly regained their composure. qQQQ popped out of his seat and crossed the room, hand outstretched, introducing himself as he went.

"Hi! qQQQ. So nice to meet you. Big fans of your show. We can't thank you enough for giving us this opportunity, and for everything you do for the 7*t*hx* scene. This is cCccc, Hh, and—"

"Nice to meet you too," interrupted M, who, after following qQQQ's introductions, was now looking directly at vV. She pulled a quick face at him as if to say, "get a load of this guy," before leading the group down the hallway and into a large soundproof booth.

vV was smitten. He had listened to M's show plenty of times, and knew her voice and sense of humour well, but he had never actually seen her before. She looked more the part of the "rock star" than any of the four of them did. Covered in tattoos and piercings, and wearing a white leather jacket, faded black band tee, white jeans, and black Docs, she made a striking figure, despite her colourful surroundings. vV caught himself with his mouth hanging open and quickly closed it, as M had done just moments before.

In a matter of seconds, the five of them were gathered around a small table, each facing a boom arm with an ElectroVoice RE20 on the end. They were each given a set of headphones, and as he put his on vV heard the outro of their latest single playing over the airwaves.

"Alright, that was c&* with 'I Need It,' here on 101.7fm. You're listening to M, and I'm sitting here with the boys in c&* as we speak! Say hello, boys."

"Hey," said qQQQ.

"Hi," said Hh.

"Hello," said vV.

"Suuup," said cCccc.

"Well, at least one of you can take directions," jabbed M, winking at vV, "Okay, let's start with the elephant in the room. What's with the name?"

"I'll take this one," said qQQQ, "When vV and I started the band together six years ago, we were both really into Black Spoon—"

"Great band," said M.

"—And they had just put out ~~AaaA~~ Blues, which we thought was absolutely badass. All the shit they were—"

"For the kids, please," interjected M.

"Sorry. All the stuff they were saying on that record about language laws was mind-blowing for us at the time, so we wanted to reflect that movement through our name."

"So, it's a political statement then?"

"Not back then it wasn't. Back then we just thought it was cool," he laughed.

"And what about now?" asked M.

"We still think it's cool," said vV.

All five of them laughed at the obvious misdirection.

"Let's move on to I Need It, then. First thing I want to know: whose '69 Impala that is on the cover? And the second thing: can you get me their number?"

More laughter.

"Hh put that one together," said cCccc.

"Yeah, it's just a cut-out from an ad in some old magazine..." said Hh.

"Well, you've got great taste, that's for sure. I understand you guys recorded the song yourselves?"

• • • •

vV doubled back into the booth, where M was still wrapping cables. He knocked gently on the door.

"Hey, I uh... you got a second?"

M looked up at him.

"Back for more?"

The interview had gone well, but in her signature fashion M hadn't made it easy for the band. Every question had come loaded with a lightning-fast rebuttal, disarming whatever ego the band had and giving vV's return to the booth an air of masochism.

"You could say that. Wanna grab a drink?" he asked.

"Now?"

"Whenever," he shrugged.

"No, I was asking. Wanna go now? I'm done here for the day."

"Oh! Fuck, well yeah, sure," laughed vV.

M went to grab her things from the staff kitchen and vV went back to the lobby to brief his bandmates, who left promptly (though not after a couple jabs of their own). When M returned to the empty room, she shot vV a look.

"Smooth," she laughed.

CHAPTER THIRTEEN

Xxxxxx had slept like shit. In fact, he hadn't slept at all. His eyelids felt weighted, and his legs were sore, making standing at his register for eight hours even less comfortable than it usually was. He had spent the previous night tossing and turning, dozing off for no longer than ten minutes at a time. He couldn't stop thinking about how profoundly M had impacted him over such a short period of time and how stupid he had been to let her into his life. This was usually followed by a spiral of embarrassment at feeling so clichéd, then anger for caring about it so much in the first place. This continued until 5am when Xxxxxx finally gave up and went to the kitchen to make himself a pot of coffee and watch the sun rise.

He noticed a spot on his uniform and began to pick at it absentmindedly.

"Some lemon juice should take that right out," said the old woman who had just pulled up to the end of his till.

Xxxxxx cursed his brain's associative prowess as images of pretzels and whiskey flashed across his vision.

"Yeah, thanks. Welcome to ~~mins~~. Will you be needing bags today?"

She proudly held up a homemade cloth shopping bag and said no, she wouldn't.

It took Xxxxxx a few seconds to recognize the thing she was holding up as a bag. It looked more like a decorative couch cushion someone had pulled all the stuffing out of. It was a gaudy floral pattern and was perfumed to match. The smell of it hit Xxxxxx right between the eyes. Floral, sure, but there was something else there too. Something sharp. Sour, even.

Bug spray, his brain told him. *It's air freshener covering the scent of bug spray.*

His head swam, and he steadied himself against the register. He felt nauseous all of a sudden. He looked out over ~~mins~~, and where once were people now stood insects of various shapes and sizes. They hissed and clicked and whined, used pincers to grab cans of beans and corn off the shelves, and pushed shopping carts with horns and legs; some resorting to throwing themselves at their cart to give it the momentum needed to move forward.

Xxxxxx looked down and saw he was an insect too. A beetle of some kind, by the looks of it. He had six tiny, saw-like arms, and a wide brown carapace. The smell of the bug spray wafted past his scent receptors, and he screamed for help. Or he meant to, anyway. What came out of his mouth was a short, sharp, tinny screech.

What the fuck is happening, he thought, panicked.

As suddenly as it had come on it all disappeared, and the elderly woman was standing in front of Xxxxxx brandishing a platinum level credit card.

"JESUS FUCK!" he screamed, clutching his now human chest. His heart felt like it wanted out. The woman shrieked.

Everyone within earshot, now thankfully also back to being people, turned to see what all the fuss was about. ffF, Xxxxxx's supervisor, came running.

"What's going on? Everything okay? Xxxxxx?"

Still catching his breath, Xxxxxx panted, "I think I'm gonna go home a little early today, if that's okay with you, boss."

ffF came around the counter and put a hand on Xxxxxxx's shoulder.

"Of course, Xxxxxxx. Of course. Do you want me to call someone? An ambulance?"

Shrugging off ffF's hand, he replied, "No, no. I'm fine. Just tired. Just tired."

That second one was for himself. Whatever had just happened was clearly something more than "just tired," but Xxxxxxx wanted none of it, whatever *it* was.

Once Xxxxxxx had steadied himself, he signed out of his register and ffF took his place serving the elderly woman, who was being consoled by Ddd a few feet away.

Xxxxxxx apologized to everyone involved and shuffled off to the breakroom, avoiding the eyes of the customers still gawking on the sidelines. He grabbed his things and got the hell out of there as quickly as he could. When he reached his car, he had an intrusive thought.

You will never have to see her again if you never come back, it said.

Xxxxxxx shook his head, but he knew it was true. He had been all-consumed by the thought of having to see M again on her next visit. What would he say? How would he react? It was largely the reason he had had so much trouble sleeping the night before, and he wouldn't be surprised if it had something to do with the episode he'd just had too.

But if he never came back, he would never have to see her again.

You need a job, jackass, came the voice of reason.

Xxxxxxx looked over his shoulder at the ~~mins~~ logo above the entrance. Some job.

He remembered M's crack about how quickly she could become his boss, and realized she had had a point, whether she had meant to make one or not. His job was devastatingly simple, and in an industry with as high a turnover rate as his, Xxxxxx's loyalty to ~~mins~~ was a golden ticket to getting a job just like it, just about anywhere.

Besides, he didn't even *like* the job. He wanted to write. And the only reason he felt he couldn't do that was because he had never done anything worth writing about. He had lived here his whole life. He had worked here his whole life. So naturally his writing reeked of *here*.

He pulled out of the parking lot and onto the highway, eastbound. When he came to his exit, he glanced down at the fuel tank indicator. What if he were to keep driving? How far could he get before running out of gas? He cut the monologue short, remembering life wasn't a 90s romcom, and took the exit.

At home, he rolled himself the fattest joint he could and kicked back in his recliner. He pulled on it, and as it smoked held it up in front of his face.

He wondered if there was something in his weed that could have caused his episode. He knew of links between schizophrenia and cannabis, but he had no history of major mental illness in his family that would lead him to consider that idea too seriously.

Could it have been cut with something? He doubted that too. This wasn't a new supply. He'd been smoking this same weed for a couple weeks now with no adverse effects, excluding the financial toll on his snack cupboard.

He took another hit. Maybe he'd just taken one too many tokes over the years, and his brain cells had given up trying to repair the damage. Did that even make any sense? He couldn't tell and laughed at the irony.

The laugh jolted him out of his reverie. Hard and hollow, it reverberated around the apartment and engulfed Xxxxxx in his own self-indulgence. The answer seemed right there in front of him, if only he could grasp it.

• • • •

"Anxiety?"

"Looks like it," said Dr bBBb.

"That seems a little... inadequate," said Xxxxxx.

"You'd be surprised. Anxiety manifests differently in everyone and can be difficult to recognize. Over time, if not properly addressed, that anxiety can build up and put unwanted stress on your system. Top that off with regular consumption of alcohol or drugs and you're playing with fire."

Xxxxxx took that in. He thought about how he craved his beer and joint at the end of a long day. How he always woke up the next morning feeling sorry for himself; hating that he had to go into ~~mins~~, counting down the hours until he could numb that feeling again at home.

He took a deep breath.

"Yes! That's it," said Dr bBBb, "slow, deep breathing is a great way to reduce your heart rate and calm your body down."

Xxxxxx exhaled.

"Thanks doc."

"For now, I'd recommend you take the next few days off work and do something you enjoy. Something relaxing. Or nothing at all. Just relax and let your body process what it needs to at its own pace. If you're still feeling off after that, we can start talking about medication. I'll write you a note for your employer, hold on."

He scuttled out of the exam room, pulling the door shut behind him.

Xxxxxxx was skeptical, but the more he thought about it the more it made sense to him. People stressed him out. It was why he hadn't gone into ~~une~~ two days ago, and it was why he had made the decision to rent an apartment in the east end. Hell, it may also be why he had never left 0xx-M-. If he couldn't handle being around nine-thousand-nine-hundred-ninety-nine other bodies, what made him think he'd have better luck in a city with ten or even one hundred times that?

He looked around the exam room. Something he had never understood about humans was how they could construct something as sturdy, yet intricate as a modern building, with all its electrical systems, plumbing, insulation, structural reinforcements, and aesthetic detailing so thought-out and mastered throughout centuries of refinement, yet couldn't always remember that eggs go on *top* of milk when packing groceries. The dichotomy boggled his mind – how people could be so smart, but also so stupid. So kind to one another, yet also so vicious. Frankly, mostly so vicious.

And I'm one, he thought miserably.

The exam room door flew open and Dr bBBb shuffled back into the room, cutting Xxxxxxx's thought short.

• • • •

Xxxxxxx never gave the note to his boss. He also never called to say he was taking a few days off. Instead, Xxxxxxx went home and began packing.

The doctor had told him to make time to relax. Xxxxxxx had decided on the way home that what he needed to "relax" was to get the hell out of dodge. He'd had enough of it here. It was time for what Xxxxxxxx wanted, and Xxxxxxx wanted to travel.

After much deliberation, he decided that if he was going to get any sort of worldview, he didn't just need to get out of 0xx-M-; he needed to get out of 9(a entirely. The next closest state was 8^a, making its capital, 3—-rr/l, the closest big city. His throat tightened at the image of tight city streets jammed with people, all individuals with their own minds and lives and thoughts and—

A lemon, Jim Beam, and pretzels supreme. A lemon, Jim Beam, and pretzels supreme, thought Xxxxxxx.

Before leaving his office, Dr bBBb had given Xxxxxxx a pamphlet full of different anxiety reducing exercises. One that had resonated with Xxxxxxx was repeating a mantra in his head to distract his brain from whatever it was that was stressing him out. Without a second thought, the cutesy, musical "a lemon, Jim Beam, and pretzels supreme" had leapt into his head.

Not wanting his mantra to be associated with the most probable cause of his mental breakdown, Xxxxxxx had spent the next ten minutes of his drive trying to come up with something better, in the end reverting to his first option out of sheer mental exhaustion.

So maybe 3—-rr/l wasn't the best option for his first destination. Due west an hour or so was 54-k7//e, a significantly smaller city. He could make his first stop there. Or, if he went east, he could stop in 7h-n9+. After that he could continue through 8^a to 7+a, and maybe even leave 0() entirely.

He decided it didn't matter. He would go as far and as long as he needed to until he wrote something worth a damn. Which direction he started in made no difference in the long run.

• • • •

As the days passed, Xxxxxxx grew quite adept at dodging phone calls from ~~mins~~. He was sure it was only a matter of time before they sent someone to check up on him, given the state he had been in when he left, but until then he would keep planning his great escape.

He had finished packing on the first day, taking with him only two bags of luggage: one large, one medium sized. Since then, he had been meticulously cancelling subscriptions, services, and anything else he could think of that might be set up for direct withdrawal from either his credit card or debit account. He was going to need every cent he had and didn't feel his Playboy Plus subscription was a priority.

He listed his apartment on the internet to be sublet and found a new tenant within fourty-eight hours. He filled in his landlord and canceled his utilities. He called everyone and everywhere he needed to to cover his ass. Everywhere but ~~mins~~, anyway.

On the fourth night, Xxxxxxx was ready. His intense drive to get out of 0xx-M- as quickly as he could had left little space in his brain to think about M, so his spirits were high when he grabbed the last beer from the fridge, one of many joints he'd rolled earlier in the day, and sat in his recliner. He patted the arm of the chair affectionately.

"Gonna miss ya, old girl," he said.

He sparked the joint and sucked back the beer, toasting the end of an era, when his phone rang. He couldn't see the microwave from where he was sitting, but common sense told him it was too late for it to be anyone from ~~mins~~. He pulled the ringing device out of his back pocket and saw it was an unknown number in a different area code. He racked his brain for what city that number correlated with. When he came up with nothing, he waited until the caller gave up and looked it up on the internet.

3—-rr/l.

Xxxxxxx didn't know anyone who lived in 3—-rr/l and all his subscriptions were canceled, so he figured it must have been a wrong number and forgot about it.

Not wanting to be disturbed any further, Xxxxxxx turned off his phone and flicked on the TV.

CHAPTER FOURTEEN

"Don't take the Chevelle, you fucking dork," laughed M.

"I just want to make a good first impression," said vV, spinning his keyring around his finger lackadaisically.

"Yeah. That's why you shouldn't show up in the Chevelle!"

They both laughed.

"Okay, okay. You're probably right. I just wanna—"

"Oh, I know what you wanna!" interjected M.

The keyring flew off vV's finger and soared in a long arc across the vestibule before smacking Pp square on the ass. The dog yelped and the pair were in stitches.

"Sorry bud!" vV squeezed out.

Pp huffed loudly and left the room.

"Okay, I'd better get going if I've gotta catch a bus," said vV, after they'd collected themselves.

He kissed M and jumped down the front steps of their home. She leaned on the door frame and watched him walk down the gravel driveway. He paused at the Chevelle, turned back towards her, and mimed a single tear running down his cheek. She flipped him off and he blew her a kiss. He continued down the road, and M watched him until he turned the corner.

vV and the band were off to the studio to track their first single under Brutal Baby Records. vV had been bouncing off the walls for the last week in anticipation of getting to track at the legendary Brutal Baby Studios, the same room all his favourite records had been cut in. M understood his excitement and was also looking forward to this day, though for entirely different reasons. If she had to hear one more mind-numbing detail about why the

LA-2A compressors in Brutal Baby's B room were superior to the ones in their A room because blah blah blah blah blah she was going to kill herself. She knew what an LA-2A was from her time at the radio station, but frankly didn't give a rat's ass what electrical components gave her voice a better "colour."

She closed the door behind her and stood out on the porch. It was a beautiful day. The sun was high in a mostly cloudless sky, save for a few fluffy cumulus clouds scattered at picturesque intervals. There was a light, cool breeze. She closed her eyes and listened to the sounds around her. Birds, cicadas, the rumble of the approaching bus on the rural route. She listened as it grew louder, slowed, and stopped. She heard a faint ping *as the doors opened, and she visualized her partner climbing aboard, dropping change into the receptacle, and taking a seat. Right on cue, she heard the tires push off the dirt road and carry vV away from her.*

She opened her eyes. The empty yard looked the same.

She took a deep breath of fresh air and decided she would finish her coffee there on the porch. She went back inside to get it, and Pp followed her back out, taking his opportunity to go for a few laps around the yard.

M laughed at the dog as it tripped over itself and faceplanted in the grass. It looked back at her with a goofy grin.

"Who's a dumbass?" she said affectionately.

Pp wagged his tail animatedly and barked once.

M sipped her coffee. Today was her day off, and she might spend the whole thing right here. Whatever chemicals raced through her system were making her feel better than she had in quite a while.

Everything seemed to be going her and vV's way lately. Both had found success in their careers, M having secured her very *own radio show and vV his band's record deal, and their home life couldn't have been better. Not to mention c&*'s latest single, Modern Lingo, was just about to be released, and with the label backing them their chance of success seemed at an all-time high.*

Pp, who had just been rolling around in the dirt on the far end of their property, leapt up suddenly, looking down the road in the direction vV had left. He began barking loudly.

"Hey! Pp! Hey, stop that!" called M.

Without warning, the blue heeler took off down the road. M went to chase after him, spilling her coffee all over her jeans as she got up, but couldn't keep up and eventually lost sight of him. She pulled her phone out and called vV, gasping for air as it rang and rang and rang, until:

"Hello?"

"vV! Pp just... took off... down the road... couldn't catch—"

"Gotcha! I can't come to the phone right now. Leave me a message and I'll get back to you eventually."

A dial tone sounded, and M furiously hung up. She hated that voicemail message, having fallen victim to it more times than she would admit to anybody.

She cursed herself for taunting the universe with her happiness, then cursed the dog for running away for no fucking reason, and finally cursed her partner for choosing the worst time to not answer his phone.

M started back towards the house. She wasn't going to catch Pp on foot, but if she took the Chevelle out she might have a better chance of finding him. So much for a nice, relaxing day off.

Back home, she changed out of her now coffee-and-sweat-stained clothes and made a quick sandwich for lunch: rye bread, butter, ham, tomato, a slice of cheese, and some romaine. She sat at the kitchen table, staring vacantly out the window as she plotted her route.

After some time, her phone rang, startling her. Without checking the number, she answered it.

"Hello?"

"Hi, is this M?" came a voice she didn't recognize.

"Yeah, that's me."

"This is the 7*t*hx* General Hospital calling. I'm afraid there's been an accident."

M's heart fell out of her chest and hit the ground with a thud.

She listened as the nurse told her a gruesome tale of a driver falling asleep at the wheel and flying through an intersection downtown, careening directly into the side of a city bus, killing three and injuring seven. The nurse struggled to find the right words to tell her that vV had been on that bus, and that he was one of the three who hadn't made it.

The kitchen melted away, and the world became as small as the speaker inside her cell phone. Everything else was a haze; a wash of formless, incommunicable sounds and colours. She didn't make a sound. She couldn't make a sound.

"Ma'am? Are you still there? Ma'am?"

M dropped the phone, which clattered loudly on the table, knocking over a mostly empty beer bottle from the night before, spilling what little was left onto the floor, but she made no indication that she saw or heard a thing. All she could hear was the faint tinny voice coming from her phone on the table, calling out "ma'am?" just once more before hanging up.

CHAPTER FIFTEEN

Xxxxxxx took one last look at his apartment in his rearview mirror.

"God damn, that's some good symbolism," he laughed.

He took off down the road and merged onto the eastbound highway. When he passed the "you are now leaving 0xx-M-" sign that marked the town limits, Xxxxxxx couldn't help but let out a triumphant yell, smacking the ceiling of his Elantra with his hand as he did so. The world was his to discover. A veritable land of milk and honey. He rolled his window down.

A few hours down the road, Xxxxxxx felt ready to think about M for the first time since his visit to the doctor's office. All that was behind him now. He had made it out. As far as he was concerned, what she had done to him paled in comparison to the fate of being left behind in 0xx-M-.

He wondered how long it would take before she realized he was gone. How many visits to ~~mins~~ would she make before it dawned on her that she wasn't just shopping on his days off? How many bags of pretzels would she eat? How many lemons? How many—?

A lightbulb appeared above Xxxxxxx's head and immediately shattered against the roof of the car, raining shards of imaginary glass all over him. Luckily, the revelation stayed intact.

Xxxxxxx slammed on the brakes and pulled onto the shoulder.

The booze. He had forgotten about the *booze.* M regularly purchased three fifths of Jim Beam every time she shopped, but

Xxxxxxx hadn't considered where all that whiskey had gone after he learned it wasn't going to ~~une~~.

He stared blankly at the steering wheel as cars flew past him.

Much like after he'd spoken to RRr, Xxxxxxx replayed every interaction he had had with M in his head, and once again saw things in a different light. She hadn't been swindling him at all. She had drunk herself dry.

Without consulting him first, his body let out a heavy sob. Then another. His hand flew over his mouth, and he closed his eyes as tightly as he could.

A lemon, Jim Beam, and pretzels supreme. A lemon, Jim Beam, and pretzels supreme.

It wasn't helping.

"NO FUCKING SHIT IT'S NOT HELPING!" he screamed, punching the steering wheel.

The sedan let out a short *honk*.

That goddamn mantra had been staring him in the face the whole time, and now the more he repeated it the more it seemed to taunt him.

A lemon, Jim Beam, and pretzels supreme! A lemon, Jim Beam, and pretzels supreme!

He broke down in tears. What had he done? At the slightest provocation he had not only deserted M when she needed him most, but he had left his hometown and cut all his ties to it. Within a *week*. One fucking week.

Forget 'what kind of friend am I?' he thought, *what kind of person am I?*

Xxxxxxx raged internally for the next fourty-five minutes, after which he found himself staring blankly out the windshield, absolutely wrecked. The sun was starting to go down and he needed to find a place to stay. He hoped his survival instincts would kick in and he would pull back onto the highway, but instead he stayed locked in position until the sun dipped below the horizon and night fell.

Never before had he so profoundly felt that he had no idea what to do with himself.

He didn't feel he deserved to sleep in a nice motel bed, and he had no bed to go home to. He had no *home* to go home to. But he also knew he couldn't stay where he was either. Any minute he expected to see that flash of blue and red come from behind him and hear that condescending tone they teach in the academy tell him he doesn't have to go home, but he couldn't stay here.

It was then that the fuel light flicked on, and Xxxxxxx realized the car had been running the whole time. That turned out to be the kick in the pants he needed.

He checked to see if anyone was coming, then pulled off the shoulder and back onto the highway. Within minutes he saw a sign for a truck stop listing a few fast-food joints, a couple gas stations, and a chain hotel. Xxxxxxx didn't love the idea of hotel room rates, but when he considered the alternative, sleeping in his car (and having to find somewhere he wouldn't get caught doing it), he decided to bite the bullet instead.

He pulled in, gassed up, and checked in at the hotel. As soon as he got to his room, Xxxxxxx pulled his cigarette tin out of his bag, grabbed a joint from inside, and took it out onto the balcony. As he took his first hit, he took in the view.

He was on the third and top floor, and while he wasn't very high off the ground the hotel was perched at the top of a large downward slope that went on for miles. Most of the landscape was taken up by densely packed trees; a dark forest that stretched on into infinity.

Xxxxxxx thought of those trees as people, each one unique in its own right, yet so uniform when viewed all at once. He wondered which tree he was.

He turned his back to the forest and looked back inside his room. He could see his translucent reflection in the sliding glass door cast over the furnishings within. His hand resting on the railing outside made it look as if he were reaching for the phone on the bedside table.

Call her, came an intrusive thought.

Before he could entertain it any further, Xxxxxxx put the thought out of his mind and ashed his smoke. He went back inside and turned on the TV before kicking off his shoes and flopping into bed.

Xxxxxxx didn't pay attention to a single thing that happened on the screen that night. While his eyes stayed trained on the TV set, his mind was off somewhere else. He needed a game plan. His original fly-by-the-seat-of-his-pants approach wasn't cutting it. He needed to decide if he was going back to 0xx-M- or continuing his journey.

Either option meant he had to find a new place and a new job on a limited budget, so it really came down to one thing: would he go back and help his friend, or finally live his life the way he'd always wanted?

Two thoughts fought for Xxxxxxx's attention. Xxxxxxx picked the one on the left. It wondered if M would even accept his help. She often dodged personal questions and wouldn't even tell him where she was staying. It wasn't a stretch of the imagination to think she might not be open to the concept of his charity. Especially if she found out he had ditched her. Besides, after this blunder he might not be in any financial state to offer charity to anybody anyway.

The second thought wrestled its way forward. It was a dark thought, but Xxxxxxx wasn't about to dismiss it either. Alcoholic or not, she *had* lied to him. That part of the story hadn't changed. Was he really willing to postpone his life any longer for someone he had only met a month ago? What did he really owe her?

Call her, came another intrusive thought.

He looked over at the phone.

"Call her," it said.

"No," said Xxxxxxx.

He took a deep breath.

We are not *talking to inanimate objects,* he thought, before wondering why he had referred to himself as "we."

"Anxiety my ass," he said.

Xxxxxxx reached into his smaller case of luggage lying open on the floor next to him and pulled out a small brown leather-bound notebook. Inside the coiled spine was a thin black pen. The pamphlet Dr bBBb had given Xxxxxxx also recommended journaling to relieve stress. While that wasn't exactly Xxxxxxx's speed, it made a good excuse to get into a daily writing routine for his poetry.

He pulled the pen out, turned off the TV, and opened the notebook to the first blank page. Where to begin?

He looked up at the now dark TV screen and saw his reflection looking back at him. He barely recognized the man.

Not that his features had changed, there was just something about the way he looked that hadn't been that way before.

Xxxxxx put the pen to paper.

Sitting on the bed
The man in the TV screen

He scrunched up his face disappointedly. His hand instinctively went to tear the page out and crumple it up, but Xxxxxx stopped it at the last second. He would keep everything he wrote in this notebook, for better or worse. No bottom drawer this time.

He looked out the window to the balcony. From that vantage point he could no longer see the parking lot in front of the hotel, only the forest in the distance. Without the context to tell his brain he was on the third floor, he could easily imagine himself much, much higher off the ground. He crossed out "the man in the TV screen" and replaced it with "high as a skyscraper," before laughing at his unintended double-entendre. Maybe he could run with that. He added the line about the man in the TV again. Now he was cooking.

Sitting on the bed
High as a skyscraper
The man in TV screen
Speaks through the telephone
He gets paid a pretty penny
To talk to suckers like me

Xxxxxx sucked on the end of his pen as he looked over what he had. It seemed promising, if a little clunky. Somehow his reflection had turned into a salesman of some kind.

And I'm like a billboard
Doing his dirty work

Because I've lost track of how many times
I've wanted to call you
And tell you all about it

Xxxxxxx smiled and shut his notebook. That would do for now. Any more and he might ruin a good thing. Better quit while he was ahead.

He stepped back onto the balcony and relit his joint from earlier. He wasn't going back to 0xx-M-. He had been out of town for less than twenty-four hours and felt he had already written what may be his best work so far. While that wasn't saying much, it was a trend he wanted to nurture. No, he *had* to nurture.

The sounds of two people having sex in the next room shook Xxxxxxx out of his head.

Great, he thought.

Xxxxxxx hadn't been laid in months, and it had been months before that too. It wasn't that he had a hard time talking to women, but that the more time he spent talking to *anyone*, male, female, non-binary, whatever, the more likely he was to be bored by them. And that could make reaching the end of a date rather difficult.

Normally a quick tug was all Xxxxxxx needed to get over himself, but knowing someone else was getting fucked for real just feet away from him was a little hard to handle. He ashed his joint, went inside to grab another, and left his room for the elevator. He was going for a walk.

The trees lining the parking lot in front of the hotel rustled in the wind.

"Caaaaaall heeeeeeeer," they whispered to Xxxxxxx.

"Fuck off, ya dumb trees," he retorted.

A mother and her young daughter were walking back inside and overheard Xxxxxx's expletive, causing the mother to double back and chastise his behavior. Xxxxxx put on his best customer service smile and apologized as sincerely as his acting skills allowed. Satisfied, the mother thanked him, extending an olive branch in the way middle-aged white women often do, likening him to "a young O;" a movie star from the 1940s.

Unsure if looking like the star of *The Man From 6t5]* was a good thing or not, Xxxxxx opted for a dry "thanks," to avoid stirring the pot any further.

Once she had returned inside, Xxxxxx lit his joint and blew it out into the trees he had just been speaking with. Two more lines popped into his head.

No movie star could hold a light to me
When I'm putting a smile on to talk to you

Joint dangling from his lips, Xxxxxx began excitedly pawing at his pant pockets looking for something to write on. When he came up dry, he exhaled heavily, and the joint popped out of his mouth. Taking it as a sign, he put what was left of it out under his shoe and headed back to his room.

By now his neighbours had gone silent, so Xxxxxx finished adding the lines to his poem, undressed, brushed his teeth, and crawled into bed.

• • • •

The next morning, Xxxxxx went down to the lobby to check out. While he waited for the concierge to finish with another patron, he flipped through a display of maps and pamphlets, hoping one might jump out at him.

He had slept surprisingly well, drifting off as soon as his head hit the pillow. When he awoke, he found himself in exactly the same position and well rested, if a little stiff. He felt ready to take on the day.

He thumbed his way through "0()'s most beautiful skylines," taking in photos of cities so impressive his brain refused to acknowledge them as real, instead dumping them in a bucket alongside concepts like Santa Claus and world peace. But they *were* real, and he was going to see them, he decided. He was going to stand in the same spot each of these photos were taken and he was going to write in each one of them. And after he did that, he would find a new brochure.

"Can I help you, sir?" came the concierge from behind him.

Xxxxxxx pocketed the pamphlet and turned.

"Uh, yeah. Just checking out. Room 306," he said.

"Perfect. How was your stay?"

"Walls were a little thin, but the view was nice."

The concierge feigned concern and apologized for the inconvenience. Xxxxxxx returned the insincerity by insisting it was no big deal and wished the man a wonderful day before returning to his car outside. Once there he pulled the pamphlet out of his back pocket. A gust of wind threatened to steal it from him and Xxxxxxx caught it at the last second. He opened the page he had snagged, displaying a nighttime shot of the 3—-rr/l Basilica. A caption below the photo explained that the basilica had taken five years to complete, starting in 1824 and ending in 1829.

Xxxxxxx wondered if there was any correlation to his own life to be made there. He needed to be careful that, in his excitement, he didn't get ahead of himself. He needed to set and keep his expectations realistic. His ride was not going to be an easy one, nor would it be a fast one. He, like the basilica, might take years to complete. This was a marathon he was living, not a sprint.

Best get started then, he thought.

He pulled out his phone and opened the maps app. If he got in a good 8 hours of driving a day, he could probably make it to the 9(a-8^a border by tomorrow evening. He still hadn't decided if he wanted his first stop to be in 54-k7//e or 7h-n9+, but based on where the highway split on the map it looked like he wouldn't have to make that decision until the end of the day.

He looked back down at the pamphlet in his other hand and wondered if he wasn't cheating himself a little. The thought of living in 3—-rr/l for any period of time caused a spike in his anxiety levels, but wasn't the whole point of his trip to actually experience the world outside of 0xx-M-? Hadn't he just pledged to visit everywhere in this pamphlet not five minutes ago?

He caught himself clenching his teeth, so he let go slowly, pocketed his phone, and massaged his jaw with his free hand.

"Fuck it. 3—-rr/l it is," he said aloud.

He crawled inside his car, which was almost unbearably hot after sitting in the summer sun all morning, rolled all the windows down, and took off down the road.

CHAPTER SIXTEEN

Across the street from the 107.7fm studio was a small pub called ~~wip~~, a bustling, loud, crowded bar populated almost exclusively by hipster-types. Every window had some version of "locally-sourced" or "organic" or "craft beer" written on it, and in front of that, spilling onto the sidewalk, was a small community garden.

M had often gotten her kicks putting up 107.7fm stickers in the bar's bathroom, only to return later in the week to find them covered with local band stickers, often with "DIY OR DIE, FUCK CORPORATE RADIO" or something of that ilk scrawled in Sharpie nearby. It wasn't that M supported corporate radio per se, but she did find it amusing to watch people get all tied up in knots about something as silly as a sticker on a bar bathroom wall.

"Ever been here?" asked vV.

"Once or twice," she replied, smirking.

"What? No good?"

"Leaves a weird taste in my mouth."

vV pulled a face.

"Shit, is the beer that bad?" he asked.

"No, not the beer," said M as she gestured with her eyes at two young hipsters walking out the front door. One of them looked M up and down, made a face as if she smelled something gross, and turned on her heels to follow her friend down the street.

"Well now we have to go in," said vV.

Inside, indie pop anthems screamed from the sound system, a volume surpassed only by the din of customers trying to have conversations overtop of it.

"What tea iguana rink?" vV asked as they approached the bar.

"What?" asked M.

"Waspy your honest ink?" he repeated.

"Oh my god," said M under her breath, before asking for clarification one more time.

"WHAT DO YOU WANNA DRINK?" screamed vV.

M laughed, throwing her head back.

"WHIS-KEY," she yelled, overenunciating as much as possible.

vV gave her a double thumbs up and ordered two whis-keys from the bar. Drinks acquired, they found a small table for two near the back of the room, serendipitously positioned behind a large beam that separated them from the nearest speaker.

"Hell of a spot," said vV, taking in his surroundings.

"You got that first part right," jabbed M.

They both laughed.

"How do you do that?"

"Do what?" asked M, genuinely confused.

vV thought about how to phrase it correctly.

"You always have the perfect reply for everything, and you seem so unfazed by everyone around you."

"Well, that's not true," said M.

"Sure, but I listen to your show all the time and—"

"Ew, am I on a date with a fan?"

"See! That! Right there!"

They both fell into stitches when the waiter came around.

"*What's so funny?*" *she asked cheerily, smacking her gum as she chewed.*

M pointed at vV.

"*This guy just asked me to marry him!*"

The waiter looked appalled by M's response to vV's alleged proposal, and her hand instinctively flew to her chest. She looked concernedly over at vV, who was still laughing hysterically. The incongruent signals warred in her neural pathways. Her brain held an emergency hearing and, lightning fast, assembled a committee to make sense of it all. One particularly bright neuron stood up, shouted, "I've got it!" and suddenly the waiter understood it was all a bit. She laughed hollowly in an attempt to save face, and quickly diverted the subject back to the task at hand.

"*Can I get you folks something to eat?*" *she asked.*

The pair shared a quick non-verbal conversation before opting out, preferring another round of whiskeys instead. vV screamed their order back to the waiter, who wasn't quite as well positioned as they were from the speaker on the wall.

After she left, vV seized his chance to change the subject.

"*So, you know your cars, eh?*"

"*Just the ones I like,*" *said M.*

"*Top choice?*"

"*Easy. '71 Chevelle.*"

"*You mean '70?*"

"*Hell naw. You heard me,*" *beamed M.*

"*No shit! I always dug the '71 too, but the guys all give me a hard time about it. Say I've got weird taste.*"

"*Well, you did pick this bar,*" *swung M.*

They laughed some more.

"Okay, my turn," said M, "If you could live anywhere you wanted, where would you go?"

"Hm... probably 3—-rr/l, if I'm being honest. What about you?"

"Whoa, whoa. Hang on. Why 3—-rr/l?" asked M.

vV chuckled uncomfortably, and M could tell he was deciding whether or not to share a vulnerable answer. Her heart warmed when he tentatively opened his mouth to speak.

"Well... my family moved a lot when I was a kid, and I travel all the time with c&*, but 3—-rr/l is just one of those places that I've never been and have always wanted to visit. It just seems so cool, from the music to the fashion to the old architecture, and I always imagined it being the place I'd move to when I was ready to hit that reset button on life. You know, settle down and start a family."

The phrase "start a family" hung uncomfortably in the air for a minute. The pair blushed at the obvious overshare for a quick drink with a stranger.

"What about you, then?" asked vV.

"I don't know, really. I've never felt the need to go anywhere else. It feels like there's a lifetime's worth of shit to do in 7*t*hx* already."

"Fair enough. As much as I love to travel, there is a certain satisfaction I get calling 7*t*hx* home. Feels like I won some sort of lottery."

"Well, it's definitely expensive enough..." said M, laughing as she rolled her eyes exaggeratedly.

The waiter returned with their whiskeys, and after more quick, non-verbal communication the pair decided they would go ahead and order a third round, too.

. . . .

M's phone would not stop ringing. Her home screen lit up with notifications of missed calls and texts from family members and friends who were one-by-one learning of vV's accident, but M paid no attention to any of them. Instead, she crashed from room to room, sobbing, violently throwing to the side any object that lay in her path, grabbing clothes, a toothbrush, her wallet, and stuffing them haphazardly into a duffel bag as she went.

She already knew how this would go. She would have to talk to vV's family, to the cops, to her friends, reliving the same horrifying story over, and over, and over. She would have to identify vV's body. There would be a funeral, everyone would line up in single file to offer her their condolences, and she would have to sit there and thank each one of them, over, and over, and over. And then she would have to come home to the same house, where she would spend every night and every morning alone.

Over, and over, and over.

Fuck that, *she thought. She was going to get out of town before anyone knew where she was headed, and she was going to get as far away from this house as possible. She was going to hit that reset button, just like vV had always wanted.*

Bag packed, she hesitated. Pp still hadn't come back since he'd run off down the street, presumably following some canine sixth sense that told him his best friend was in trouble (he had always liked vV best). The thought of losing both her guys on the same day caused her to double over into another sobbing fit. She put her hand on the wall to steady herself. Her head swam, but she knew her window of opportunity was already starting to shut. She didn't have time to grieve. She didn't have time to weigh *her options. If she stood a chance of getting out of 7*t*hx* before anyone noticed, she had to leave* now.

Her abdominals ached. Her head pounded. She couldn't think straight.

She threw open the front door and stepped out onto the patio. There it was. That gorgeous piece of machinery that she had convinced vV not to take to the studio. That fine feat of engineering that they had both lusted after for so many years. That 1971 Chevelle SS with one hell of an engine that now sat as motionless as its owner, wherever he was now. There was no way in hell she was taking that car.

She felt another pang of grief in her chest, gulped it down, steeled herself for a moment, and went around to the back of the house.

Leaning up against the side of the house was M's old Schwinn, which she yanked out of the undergrowth snaking its way around the spokes. She hadn't ridden it in months and wondered if it even had any air left in the tires. A quick squeeze found two surprisingly full tubes, so she hopped on the worn leather saddle and tore down the dirt road towards the Greyhound station, listening intently for the sounds of a blue heeler the whole way.

CHAPTER SEVENTEEN

A single raindrop fell on the windshield of Xxxxxxx's Elantra as he approached a tall hill. He leaned forward in his seat to get a better look at the sky. He had been eyeing some angry looking clouds in the distance shortly after he had left the hotel that morning, and it seemed they were finally above him.

As if on cue, a swath of darkness fell over the horizon and rushed towards Xxxxxxx. In seconds it enveloped him, and the car's automatic headlights flickered on. Seconds after that, a sheet of rain followed suit and Xxxxxxx found himself in the middle of a downpour.

Xxxxxxx turned on the windshield wipers to their highest speed. They whipped left and right, flinging buckets of water off the side of the car, which met with the water kicked up by the tires, ricocheting wildly in tandem with the soaring vehicle and creating a dense mist behind him. Despite the wipers working at full capacity, Xxxxxxx could barely see twenty feet in front of him. He applied the brakes slowly to avoid hydroplaning, eventually getting down to a cool 60km/h as he crested the hill.

He let out a breath he hadn't realized he'd been holding when a pickup truck with its brights on came roaring over the top of the hill, practically on top of him, and landed with its front bumper on the trunk of his car. There was a deafening crash. The truck's headlights flooded the interior of the sedan, reflecting off the rearview mirror directly into Xxxxxxx's eyes, blinding him. The truck veered left, pushing the Elantra right, and bounced back onto the road with the help of the latter's suspension. Without slowing, the pickup screamed into the night, leaving behind nothing but burnt rubber tracks on the pavement. The Elantra flew off the road and into the ditch, knocking Xxxxxx around like a rag doll. His head knocked forward against the steering wheel, then snapped sideways against the door, then straight back into the seatbelt retractor. The hood of the car met the trunk of a deep-rooted oak and caved in the front end of the car to match the back. Xxxxxx's vision blurred from the edges to a fine point, and his senses dulled as he passed out.

When the dust finally settled, his senses slowly returned to him. First, his eyes cracked open, adjusting in slow motion. Indistinct shapes gained form – sharpened around the edges. Then his hearing returned, as if a heavy blanket was slowly being pulled from over his ears.

One by one his surroundings came into focus. When he gained his confidence, Xxxxxx gingerly raised his hand and began assessing the damage to his person.

His clothes were pulled in all kinds of funny and uncomfortable ways, but thankfully he seemed relatively unscathed, save for a bloody nose and a cut on the back left of his head where it had bounced off the seat belt retractor.

The car was stuck on an angle, pulled down into the mud by the tree, the back left tire completely off the ground. Despite the bent frame, the driver side door still opened as intended, so Xxxxxx crawled from the wreckage and out into the rain. Within seconds he was soaked and freezing. He reached for his phone in his back pocket just in time to see his home screen go black as it either shorted from the rain, ran out of battery, or just generally gave up after being run off the road by a pickup.

In a rage, Xxxxxxx tossed it into the woods next to the road and immediately regretted it. Not that it was any help to him dead, his phone was still his only connection to the outside world.

He knew he would never find his phone in the deluge, so he cut his losses and went back up to the road to try and flag someone down. On his way out of the ditch, he slipped in the wet grass and fell face first into the mud. Cursing, he tried again and met the same fate. As he got up to try a third time, he saw a flash of light on the horizon as a car climbed the hill. He pushed off the muddy earth with as much force as he could muster, frantically trying to reach the road in time. Of course, this only made him slip again, and he let out a cry as the headlights came into view and drove right by without seeing him or the wreckage.

Defeated, Xxxxxxx crawled back to the Elantra and pulled open the rear driver-side door. He pulled himself inside the vehicle, smearing mud all over the upholstery, and lay on his stomach in the now caved-in backseat.

He closed his eyes and lay there for a moment, listening to his surroundings. All he could hear now was the rain tap-tap-tapping incessantly on the roof of the totaled sedan. Otherwise, all was eerily still.

Then, as if nothing had happened at all, the rain stopped, and the sun returned. Light poured in the back window and right into Xxxxxxx's eyes, warming his face. He squinted, and suddenly burst into laughter.

He laughed so hard the car began to shake with him, metal rubbing against metal in a way that made it seem like the car was in on the joke. He laughed until tears streamed down his cheeks and his abdominals ached. He laughed until he couldn't bear to laugh any longer, and then laughed some more.

He had tempted the universe, and the universe had called his bluff. Now the cards were down, and he was living, alright. He was living in that way he had only read about in his favourite books. Had only fantasized about. That kind of living that's so goddamn awful you have to look at it poetically, or risk losing your mind entirely. That kind of living that you learn to look back on affectionately – if only because you can say you made it out alive. He was stranded on a highway somewhere deep in 9(a with a totaled car, no phone, no food, no one looking for him, no one expecting him, and not a whole lot in the bank. If he was going to make it, he was going to have to do it himself. And then he would write the most interesting, insightful, powerful work anyone had ever written. Goddamn right.

"HEY! ANYBODY IN THERE?" called a booming voice from the road.

Xxxxxxx perked up and rolled over. While he may have been ready to take on the world all by himself, he wasn't against getting a little help either. He sat up and awkwardly shimmied his way back out the door he had crawled in moments earlier. The sun was warm on his body, and he could feel himself drying immediately.

"HEY BUDDY, YOU ALRIGHT?"

Before Xxxxxxx could answer, a massive barrel-chested redhead in overalls came bounding towards him. He wrapped his arm around Xxxxxxx's waist and helped him out of the sideways car. When they were both upright, Xxxxxxx shook him off.

"I'm okay, really. Thank you."

The man took a step back and looked Xxxxxx up and down.

"Boy, you look fuckin' aw-ful."

"Thanks," said Xxxxxx dryly.

The man let out a hearty laugh.

"Alright, let's get you outta here."

He gestured with his thumb over his shoulder, and Xxxxxx noticed the hook-and-chain tow truck on the road behind him. A big, white beast to match its owner. On the side was a simple red and black logo that read: "TtttT's Towing."

"She's a beaut, eh?" he asked.

"Sure," said Xxxxxx.

"Yup, first truck I ever bought. Been with me through thick and thin, she has."

The man planted his feet and put his hands on his hips as he looked lovingly at the vehicle, no doubt as a montage of happy memories played inside his head. Xxxxxx watched him, amused.

Eventually, the man, whose name turned out to be TtttT, rigged up the Elantra and helped Xxxxxx salvage what was left of his luggage, wedging it behind Xxxxxx's headrest in the cramped tow truck. He kept repeating how lucky Xxxxxx was that he had been driving past that day and that he should thank his lucky stars or whatever deity (he pronounced it "ditty") he prayed to.

When the two were back on the road, Xxxxxx explained everything that had happened, from the sudden storm to the pickup that ran him off the road, and TtttT spent much of the next hour very sweetly calling that pickup driver every nasty name in the book, wishing them the fieriest of deaths in the most colourful language he was capable of.

As they drove to the next town, Xxxxxxx found himself warming to TtttT. Loud, obnoxious, and overbearingly kind-hearted, he may as well have been the Dr Hyde to Xxxxxxx's Jekyll, but he was also so unabashedly honest Xxxxxxxx couldn't help but find him something special.

"Man, you ever wonder how much a porn star gets paid?" asked TtttT out of the blue.

Xxxxxxx burst out laughing. Not because he thought the subject matter was particularly funny, but that it was the first thing that had come out of either of their mouths in the last fifteen minutes and it made for one hell of an icebreaker.

"No idea, how much?" said Xxxxxxx.

"Shit, I dunno. Just askin'."

Xxxxxxx burst into laughter again.

"You sure are giggly." said TtttT.

Xxxxxxx didn't reply. He was tired and couldn't think of anything to say. Luckily for him, his participation in the conversation turned out to be optional.

"But like I's sayin', how much do you think? Like, are we talkin' six figures, you think? I mean girls like YyYy, you know? Yeeeeah, you know! Chicks like that. What's she pullin' in at the end of a physical year, you think?"

Xxxxxxx marveled at TtttT's ability to ask so many questions while simultaneously leaving no time to possibly answer them. It was truly a work of art. Every so often he would slip up on a word, like using "physical" when he meant "fiscal," but he would always confidently breeze past it and be on to the next thing before Xxxxxx had time to catch the mistake.

As TtttT's voice faded into the background, Xxxxxxx took in his surroundings. They were just coming into the next town. Coming up on the right was a large junkyard.

An idea jumped into his head.

"Hey TtttT," interrupted Xxxxxxx.

TtttT stopped talking mid-sentence and turned his attention to Xxxxxxx. Cutting him off was just about the only way to get him to shut up, so he rarely took it personally. Instead, he lifted his eyebrows to signal he was listening.

"How much do you think my car would go for at a place like that?" asked Xxxxxxx.

"That hunk o' crap? I'd say hundred-fifty, two-hundred maybe."

"Would that cover you?"

"Come again?" said TtttT.

"Would that be enough to cover the tow job? You know, accounting for the time we've got left to go."

TtttT thought about it for a moment.

"Just about."

"Good enough. Pull over."

"What, you're serious? You're crazy, man."

Xxxxxxx insisted, and TtttT pulled over.

Xxxxxxx popped out the passenger side of the tow truck and crossed the lot to the office at the other end. He had to admit he liked the way it felt when TtttT called him crazy. The way he said it carried a certain level of respect, maybe even a subtle envy. Xxxxxxx had always been "kind," or "funny," or "considerate," but he had never been "crazy." He puffed out his chest and walked into the office.

• • • •

TtttT was woken up by a loud *smack*! He groggily looked around the cabin of the truck and found Xxxxxxx staring right at him, holding a thick white envelope. He smacked it on the dash one more time.

Smack!

"Wus... wusgoinon..?" grumbled TtttT.

"Two-fifty!" said Xxxxxxx enthusiastically.

"I don... wushappening?"

Xxxxxxx gave TtttT a minute to fully wake up before explaining to him how he had talked the junkman into selling him his Elantra for two-hundred-and-fifty dollars, not the two hundred TtttT had suggested earlier. Now able to understand Xxxxxxx's excitement, TtttT mirrored it as best as his melatonin-soaked brain would allow.

"No shit! Atta boy."

He gave Xxxxxxx's shoulder a hearty slap before looking around the cabin. The sun was starting to go down, the sky a bright pink. It cast a glow over everything in sight.

"How long was I out for?" he asked.

"Long enough for me to make a deal and junk a car," replied Xxxxxxx.

TtttT looked at his rearview mirror and, sure enough, the Elantra was gone. He had slept right through the whole ordeal.

"Jeee-zus! Guess I needed a little shuteye, eh?"

"Guess so. And speaking of which, do you think we'll be in town soon? I've still got to find a place to crash and—"

"Oh yeah! We're practically there now. As for where you're crashin', you're welcome to stay with ol' TtttT if ya like."

Xxxxxxx thought about it for a minute. He liked the idea of a free couch, and had no issue spending more time with TtttT, but after the day he had had all he really wanted was a room and a comfortable bed to himself. He thanked TtttT for the offer and said he would find a motel instead.

"Your loss!" said TtttT with a chuckle as he pulled back onto the road.

Within minutes, they were in town. A wooden sign greeted them as they passed: "Welcome to 8ui::v – 9(a's blueberry capital!" They passed under a bridge and entered a quaint stretch of road lined with wooden fencing painted blue and purple, presumably to mimic the colours of a blueberry.

TtttT pointed to a building farther down the street.

"There's yer motel," he said, "Just gotta drop ya off at the shop first to sort out some paperwork."

X looked down at the wad of cash in his lap.

"What if I just gave you this and we called it even?"

TtttT laughed powerfully, shaking the entire truck.

"You're a crazy fucker, ya know that? You got a deal."

He stuck out a massive hand, eyes still locked on the road, and they shook on it. TtttT dropped Xxxxxxx at the motel, and Xxxxxxx left the envelope on his seat as he hopped out. They said a rather heartfelt goodbye for a pair of strangers and went their separate ways.

The motel was on a tiny plot of land, squished between a pizza place and an apartment building. It looked like the definition of an afterthought, everything slightly askew as if the entire building had been wedged in between the other two by a giant.

Xxxxxxx walked in the front door. A small bell tinkled above his head.

A teenage girl dressed in a baggy plaid flannel shirt and camouflage cargo pants sighed dramatically and shut the book she was reading.

"Hey," said Xxxxxxx, "got a room for the night?"

"Ya. One sec."

She tapped wildly on a keyboard attached to an ancient desktop computer, spun around in her chair, grabbed a key from the back wall, spun back towards Xxxxxxx, and pointed to the debit machine.

"When you're ready."

Through this entire exchange, she moodily avoided direct eye contact. Xxxxxxx wondered if it was an intimidation tactic, or genuine apathy.

He put the thought out of his mind, inputted his information, got his key, and went to his room on the second floor. Regardless her reason, he was grateful. It beat having to explain to her why he looked like a swamp monster.

The stairs protested as he climbed them, some bending slightly too far underfoot for comfort. When he reached the landing, he was face-to-face with the door to his room. The hall stretched down to his right, ending in a floor-to-ceiling mirror. Xxxxxxx waved at his bloodied reflection down the hall before entering.

He flicked on the light and jumped as a pair of black rats, each the size of a small dog, ran for cover. Suddenly he missed the comparative swank of his previous room, neighbours and all. He cringed as the thought went out to tempt the universe and snatched his hand in the air as if he could pull it back before it accidentally manifested.

He looked over at the bed. The sheets looked permanently stained and stretched well beyond anything Xxxxxxx could call "worn out."

If I 'manifest' anything tonight, it's going to have to be a version of myself willing to sleep in that fucking thing, he thought.

Opting to leave his shoes on, he pulled the plain wooden chair out from behind a small desk blocking the fire escape in the back corner. He removed his ruined shirt and used it as a rag to wipe a thick layer of dust off the chair. Safer to sit here than anywhere more recently disturbed, he figured.

After replacing his old shirt with a cleaner one (nothing he had was fully clean anymore), he sat in the chair and pulled out his notebook; the one thing in the wreckage he refused to leave behind.

It was so thoroughly drenched that, while drying, the bottom third of every page had warped. He opened it gently, the pages crackling. His poem from the previous night was mostly washed away. All he had left was:

Sitting on the bed
High as a skyscraper
The man in TV screen
Speaks through the telephone
He gets paid a pretty penny
To talk to suckers like me
And I'm like a billboard

He scratched his head, trying to remember the rest. He remembered bits and pieces, but not exact phrases. He cursed.

His brain felt foggy. He really wanted to smoke. While he had found his notebook in the rubble earlier that day, Xxxxxxx hadn't been so lucky with his weed.

He remembered something about putting a smile on after the woman who had said he looked like a young O. That was a start. But what was this about a billboard? What wild tangent had his drug-addled brain been leading him on?

Eventually Xxxxxxx gave up trying to remember what he had initially written and shut the notebook. His stomach grumbled loudly. He tried and failed to remember the last time he had eaten, and – like Wile E. Coyote when he's suddenly realized he's run off a cliff – he suddenly felt weak with hunger. He welcomed an excuse to leave his dirty motel room and walked out into the street to find something to eat. To his left upon exiting was the pizza place he had seen earlier. He popped in for a slice or six.

The teenager at the register looked mortified as soon as he saw Xxxxxxx walk in. His eyes went wide, and he stood straight up, doing his best to avoid eye contact while still trying to steal glances whenever he thought Xxxxxxx wasn't looking.

The shock of finding two gargantuan rodents in his motel room had rattled Xxxxxxx enough that he had forgotten to wash up before he left. He reached up and felt the back of his head, still crusted with blood from where it had hit the seat belt retractor, and empathized with the poor kid. Between that and his bloody nose, which had no doubt dried all down his face by now, Xxxxxxx must have looked like patient zero in the zombie apocalypse.

When he reached the till, Xxxxxxx eyed the menu up and down, taking his time as the kid squirmed. No one said a word for a full minute.

"I'll have two slices of pepperoni, and one Hawaiian, please," said Xxxxxxx.

"Are you okay?" asked the kid, whose nametag read "wwWwW."

"Wear a seatbelt," said Xxxxxxx dryly.

wwWwW's eyes widened even further for a fraction of a second.

"Oh my god," he said.

"I'm fine. Just have to shower."

They both stared at each other for a few seconds longer before Xxxxxxx broke the silence.

"Hey man, I'd love that pizza."

The kid jumped out of his skin. His skeleton tapped frantically on the register before turning and shuffling awkwardly over to the oven with his fleshy bits wrapped around his ankles. He reached down and pulled his skin back over his body like a jumpsuit before tossing two slices of pepperoni – and one Hawaiian – into the oven.

Xxxxxxx paid for his food and moved over to the far wall to wait while his dinner heated. When wwWwW returned with his slices, they were already all boxed up for him. The subtle suggestion that he not eat-in was not lost on Xxxxxxx.

Xxxxxxx grabbed his food and left the shop. The thought of eating in his motel room made him sick, so he scarfed down the pizza on the curb out front instead, smiling and waving at all the people that stared as they passed. They looked terrified. He didn't care.

"Who you are isn't how you feel, though. It's all about who you know. The people around you decide what kind of person you are."

He remembered M's words back at ~~mon~~, what felt like a lifetime ago now. To all these people he was a certifiable nutcase, bloodied, hunched over a box of pizza on a curb in a town he couldn't even remember the name of, eating as if it was his last meal.

Ever since that fateful lunch he had felt himself slowly unraveling, and now he wondered how much more there was left to unravel. The thought spooked him.

Good, he thought, *if I'm scared it means I've still got something to lose.*

He wriggled his nose in distaste. True as it was, he still had hated clichés.

PART THREE
CHAPTER EIGHTEEN

M woke up with her head pounding. Nothing new, she reached down for her flask and took a swig to take the edge off. Her head throbbed powerfully, and she passed out again.

When she woke up the second time she was confused. Usually that did the trick. Her senses sharpened slowly, and she realized she couldn't open her right eye. She brought her hand up to touch it and found it swollen shut. Gradually, the memory of her tripping into the corner of the desk came back and it all started to make sense.

She sat up slowly, taking extra care to not make any sudden movements. Her depth perception seemed a little skewed, though not terribly. She turned, fell on all fours, and crawled to the foot of the bed, using it to get upright. Suddenly, her sense of urgency returned. She couldn't remember why she had to get out, but that she had to get out *now.*

Next to her on the bed was her packed duffel bag. She grabbed it and went for the door, taking extra care to grab her last half-full bottle of whiskey off the floor as she went. With every step her memory returned, giving more and more context to her hurried exit, until she was out the door and across the road, entirely caught up. She sprinted as far as she could go, which turned out not to be very far, before settling into a brisk walk. When the Greyhound platform that welcomed her first steps into 0xx-M- was out of sight she relaxed slightly. She would still need to keep an eye out, but figured she was mostly in the clear now.

After twenty-five minutes, a car finally passed that wasn't heading towards 0xx-M-. While the summer sun stayed high in the sky, M figured it must have been around five o'clock when she left. All those commuters that worked in the city were returning home to their families for dinner, which meant the motel would be expecting to hear from her any time now.

The approaching car was a beat-up blue Saturn. M stuck her thumb out. The car slowed as it passed and pulled over. She jogged up to the passenger-side window as it rolled down.

"Hey man! Can you give me a ride?" she asked.

The man behind the wheel looked her up and down. He appeared to be in his mid- to late-thirties, and to have once or twice dabbled in methamphetamines. He tipped his ripped mesh, unbranded ball cap at her.

"Where ya headed?" he asked.

"Where ya goin'?" she replied.

The man smiled toothlessly.

"2^:bb. 'Sup with yer eye?"

"Tripped. Got space in your trunk?"

"Yuuuup."

He pulled a lever under his seat and the trunk flew open. She tossed in her duffel bag, shutting it on her way to the passenger side door.

Not seconds after she'd put on her seatbelt, the man floored it and they soared back onto the road. They merged onto the highway going a brisk 145km/h, and M began to wonder if this was to be her fate. To die in a fiery car crash, just like—

"WOOOOOOHOOOOOO!" cried the man.

He slowed down to the speed limit, having gotten whatever that was out of his system.

"How'd ya like THAT?" he screamed at M, spittle flecking her face.

"How'd I like what?"

He looked dejected. M supposed that was his move. Some sort of dominance thing. She knew the type. She was sure he'd start calling her names any second now.

Instead, he said "whatever," and sat in sullen silence for the next few minutes.

M took the chance to enjoy her surroundings. Pine trees flew by, lining both sides of the two-lane highway. The sky was clear, and M saw a handsome hawk circling them overhead. She took a nip of whiskey.

"Hey, can I have some of that?" asked the man.

"You're driving," said M.

"Just a sip. Tiny sip," he bargained.

"No. It's all I've got."

He grumbled the word "bitch" under his breath but left it at that.

M was getting all kinds of bad feelings from this guy. He kept fidgeting and picking obsessively at a spot on his jeans. He radiated a dangerous, anxious energy.

Her stomach sank, and she wondered if she had made the wrong choice by getting in this man's car.

Jeez, when you put it that *way,* she thought to herself.

The two of them remained in silence for another ten minutes before M asked if he would mind turning on the radio.

"Don't want to talk to me?" he asked, fake pouting.

"Man," said M, and nothing more.

She knew better than to prod a guy like this. She had already seen enough to bet he couldn't take a joke. She sat silently and did her best not to exacerbate his mood.

Neither of them said anything for the next hour and a half when signs for 2^:bb started becoming more frequent. The sun was setting, casting an orange glow over everything in sight. The man pulled off the highway and snaked his way down a series of nondescript gravel roads and farmland until they got into town. He drove down the main street, passing franchised chain restaurants and bargain retailers, each one looking as rundown as the last. At the far end of the main drag was a small park, and behind that were rows of houses where the residential part of town began.

"You can drop me off right here," said M.

"What do you mean, right here? What's here?" said the man, waving his arms around.

"Just let me out, please."

He pulled over, and M got out.

"Hey, thanks for the ride. I appreciate it. Pop the trunk?"

"Gas, grass, or ass," was the man's reply. He said it slowly, as if he liked the way the words felt in his mouth and wanted to savour them.

"Excuse me?"

"Did I stutter?"

M walked around the front of the car; eyes locked with the man the whole time. He grinned stupidly, showing rows of rotted teeth, few as they were. When she reached the driver's side, she bent over to look him in the eye. He brazenly looked down at her chest, then back up to meet her gaze.

"Gas, grass, or ass," he repeated, "if you want your bag."

M turned an idea over in her mind, steeling herself. She bit her lip. He giggled excitedly. Through the open window of the Saturn, she slid her finger down his chest, all the way to his belt buckle. She paused.

"That's it, baby" cooed the man encouragingly.

In one swift motion, she balled her hand into a fist and punched the man in the crotch as hard as she could. He cried out in pain and doubled over, both hands flying to cover himself in case she wanted another shot. M reached behind his head and brought his face into the steering wheel as hard as she could. His reflexes rocked his head back as blood spouted from his nose. She pulled the car door open and yanked the lever by the man's feet to open the trunk. She felt his hands grabbing for her, his fingers sliding through her hair, but they couldn't get a good enough grip and within seconds she was out of his reach. She grabbed her bag and sprinted across the park.

Already winded, she looked around her for a place to hide, swiveling her head wildly to compensate for her lack of peripheral vision. At the far end of the park, at the back end of someone's lot, was a tall hedge. She used what little energy she had left and ran straight for it. She pressed herself into the bush as far as she could and fell silent, doing her best to hold her breath as she listened to the sounds of the evening.

At the other end of the park, she heard the man howling, calling her a bitch over and over. She saw a woman cross the street in the distance.

Eventually, the man calmed down and she heard him slam the trunk closed before tearing off into the night. She finally caught her breath and lay down in the grass to rest for a moment. Within seconds she was asleep.

• • • •

Miraculously, no one passed by the whole night, save for a skunk and a family of inquisitive raccoons, neither of which disturbed the exhausted, drunken M enough to wake her. When she opened both her eyes, which was a relief unto itself, she was still pressed into the dirt under the shadow of the tall hedge. She reached for her phone to check the time and saw it had died at some point overnight. It was only a matter of time before her service would be cut off anyway, but she had been hoping to use the device until then. She cursed and sat up.

The sun was already high in the sky. She attempted to gauge the time based on its location and decided it was probably sometime between seven and eleven o'clock.

Real helpful, she thought.

Her stomach grumbled loudly. She hadn't eaten since lunchtime the day before and needed to find something to eat pronto. She recalled the chain restaurants back on the main drag, but knew she had no money to buy anything. She supposed that meant she would have to panhandle or dumpster-dive.

She crawled back out onto the sidewalk and made her way up to the main street. A few people were out walking their dogs, but the streets seemed relatively quiet. M considered this against her two options and ducked into the alley behind the first establishment. She didn't feel her odds of finding something edible were great after the critters of the night had gotten first dibs, but she also didn't think she was likely to get any worthwhile cash from a few dogwalkers either.

Her head pounded, but she didn't reach for her flask. She knew better than to drink on this empty of a stomach. She would have to find food first, then take care of her hangover.

She popped open the first dumpster and found nothing but cardboard and clear plastic clothes hangers. The next two were the same. The third was filled with black garbage bags but smelled so awful M couldn't bear the thought of eating from it and immediately shut the lid.

On she went down the line of stores, until she came upon a bakery. The dumpster was locked, likely to prevent the aforementioned critters from getting inside, but there was a round opening in the top M bet she could snake her arm through. With a much larger wingspan than your average raccoon, she was able to reach down into a veritable sea of stale croissants and danishes. She shoveled them into her mouth ravenously, coughing whenever the flaky pastry dried out her throat. She reached into her back pocket and took a swig from her flask to wash it down. Her headache washed away with it.

Satiated, she swung herself onto her backside and sat on the edge on the dumpster for a moment, swinging her dangling feet. She looked around the alleyway.

What a peculiar situation this is, she thought. She had no idea where she was and was hardly itching to flag another ride down after her experience the night before, but she knew she had to go *somewhere.* She had vowed to make it to 3—-rr/l. She had to. Non-negotiable.

She took a deep breath, hopped onto the pavement, and walked back out onto the street. The bakery's storefront was bustling, which surprised her, having entered the back alley in a ghost town, and her heart rate quickened when she realized how risky her breakfast had been. That thought was followed by another that told her all these people were paying three dollars a pop for croissants much like the ones she had just gorged on for free, and that made her feel a little better.

M looked through the window and met eyes with a baby watching her over its mother's shoulder. She crossed her eyes and stuck out her tongue, and the baby giggled. The mother looked down at the baby, then back out the window at M. When she saw the dirty, pierced face that had been interacting with her child, she turned the baby away from the window and shot a disapproving look in its direction.

M uncrossed her eyes, only to roll them back in her head, open her mouth, and stick out her tongue as far as she could. The woman looked terrified. M laughed and continued to walk down the street. She felt more like herself that morning, and a sliver of hope returned to her disposition.

She passed a young man in pink shorts and a navy-blue t-shirt walking his retriever.

"Excuse me, is there a train or bus station anywhere around here?" she asked.

The man pulled a pair of earbuds out of his ears, and M repeated her question. He thought about it for a moment before saying he was "pretty sure there's a Greyhound station off Fern." M asked if Fern was a street name or code for something and the man said it was the former. She got directions and thanked him for his help.

She glanced down at the panting retriever and was returned to her porch in 7*t*hx*, watching Pp bark wildly at nothing before taking off down the street.

The retriever sensed her inner turmoil and whined sympathetically. It walked up to her and nudged her hand with its head. M looked at the man, who nodded, before she crouched to pet the dog.

"Good boy," she whispered. She didn't risk using her vocal cords for fear of her voice breaking.

Tears welling up in her eyes, she nodded a thank you to the man and left swiftly in the direction of Fern Street.

She found the bus station with relative ease. She knew she couldn't afford a ticket, but if she was near a station of some kind, she was likely also near a main road where she might be able to intercept travelers passing by, which turned out to be exactly what she did. She was nervous to get into another stranger's car but couldn't think of any better options that cost nothing and preserved her anonymity.

For the remainder of that day, she hopped from ride to ride, selectively opting for female drivers or families that were feeling brave enough to pick up a leather-clad punk like her. This proved difficult to maintain and eventually she began accepting rides from men as well, though trusting her gut whenever it told her not to ride with someone. By the end of the second day her head was full of pop radio hits and her clothes smelled like moldy takeout containers, secondhand smoke, and a few other odors M didn't, and didn't want to, recognize.

With every ride came a new personality, and M began to miss the rapport she had had with Xxxxxxx. While none of these people were nearly as slow as the man she had caught her first ride with, they weren't quite on M's level either. Eventually, she learned to find satisfaction in the sound her jokes made when whizzing over their heads, but that satisfaction paled in comparison to the rush of having a real competitor to spar with.

One afternoon, right after crawling out from the back of a suburban family's SUV with remarkably little leg room, she found a twenty-dollar bill stuck in the mud. Glancing down at her aching stems, she noticed the sun reflecting off one of the bill's holograms, catching her eye like some sort of celestial allowance. The pastries she had eaten earlier hadn't sustained her for very long, and while the odd driver would offer her snacks like trail mix or dried fruit, she was far from full.

In an effort to make the bill last as long as possible she opted for a bag of pretzels from the first corner store she passed, eating slowly, savouring each bite. She washed it down with a nip of Jim Beam.

She passed a bench and sat on it, facing a small playground next to a baseball diamond. Behind that was a small elementary school.

She doubted she would have much luck sleeping outside that night. There were houses all around, and she didn't want to risk having someone call the cops on her. Besides, it had rained earlier that day and the grass was damp.

M flapped her lips exasperatedly. She could have been on the other side of the planet and no more lost than she felt right there on that bench. She took another swig from her flask. It was starting to feel empty, so, after making sure the coast was clear, she filled it with the remainder of the bottle in her duffel bag.

"Home stretch," she said to no one.

She continued down the street until she came to a main road. She snuck behind a closed office supply store and found exactly what she had been hoping for: an industrial sized recycling bin. She popped the top open and crawled inside, rearranging deconstructed cardboard boxes and reams of discarded paper into a makeshift bed. She pulled the lid shut and imagined herself a vampire closing the lid on her coffin.

I vont to sell you ovvice supplies! she thought to herself. She didn't laugh. It wasn't that good of a joke.

CHAPTER NINETEEN

When Xxxxxx returned to his motel room he stripped down and walked straight into the shower. He put his head under the stream and watched as red poured in dancing rivulets from the ends of his hair onto the shower floor like rain running off a gutter.

What a day, he thought, chuckling at the understatement.

When he finished washing himself, he grabbed his pile of clothes from outside the shower and washed those too. He would wash the rest of what he had salvaged another time. For now, he just needed something to wear.

He got out of the shower and hung his clothes up to dry. The air was thick with moisture from his shower, and he quickly realized he would have to take his clothes outside the bathroom if he expected them to dry any time before next week.

Still naked, he grabbed his wrung-out underwear, socks, jeans, and t-shirt and carried them into his moldy motel room. He spun on the spot a few times looking for a place to lay them down that didn't look like it should come with a disclaimer.

He bunched all his clothes in his left hand and used his right to pull the comforter off the bed, tossing it on the floor. The sheet underneath was stained in a few places, but they looked like old stains, washed and rewashed so many times that they had faded in a gradient to the original white around the edges. He lined his damp clothes along the side of the bed he didn't intend to sleep on, far enough that the wet wouldn't seep to his side during the night.

He didn't want to touch anything until he at least had some underwear on, so he grabbed his notebook and stood in the middle of the room, stark naked, as far from everything as he could get. He opened the book to his work-in-progress poem and stared at the one line whose origins had eluded him the previous night.

And I'm like a billboard

He crossed out "billboard." He didn't feel he was advertising much these days. He started jotting down words in the margins to describe how he felt a bit more aptly.

crazy

lost

alone

He stared at the three words he had just written and fought back tears. Those three words seemed to sum up a lot of how he had felt his whole life. No one had ever truly been in his corner. When he was younger, he had always had the "odd" or "quirky" viewpoint none of his classmates could quite grasp. Always the weirdo. Always the underdog.

He turned to a fresh page and began writing.

the perfect underdog
the consummate dark horse
is like a seed in the mud
working 9-5 at a dead-end job.
the perfect underdog
the consummate dark horse
gets paid by the hour
to reward the risky bidder.
the perfect underdog
the consummate dark horse

turns into the flower
when the sun goes down.

Xxxxxx exhaled heavily. He was the perfect underdog. He was the consummate dark horse. He was a blank slate.

No matter where he went now, no one would have any preconceptions about him, or would know, or *care* to know, anything about him. From here on out, he *was* Xxxxxx the writer, if he wanted to be. His past was his own to redefine.

He decided to start his new history with underwear on. His legs were tired, and he wanted to lie down. His boxers were still a little damp, but he figured his body heat would dry them soon enough.

He walked over to the motel window and pulled open the curtain. His second floor view over 8ui::v was surprisingly nice, and he smiled. He opened the window to let in the sound of the crickets and the fresh air and crawled into bed. Exhausted, he fell asleep immediately.

• • • •

Xxxxxx woke up drenched. He cursed. His clothes must have been wetter than he thought when he laid them out the night before. It wasn't until the salty odor of sweat hit his nose that he realized the wet was coming from him. He sat up.

He had sweat right through the sheet and the bedspread beneath it, capillary action making the outline of his body look like a bloated crime scene chalk drawing.

Just great, he thought, *I wet the fucking bed. Bad underdog.*

He hopped back in the shower to rinse off. When he got back out, his head started to throb dully. He really hoped he hadn't caught something.

He toweled off and got dressed. It was 8:37am, so he still had plenty of time to get breakfast before he had to check out.

At the front desk, the surly teenager who had checked him in had been replaced by a kind-faced older man in a red and blue plaid shirt, who jovially greeted Xxxxxxx when he walked around the corner. He looked to be in his sixties, his hair greyed, but with the faintest shimmer of its former black still underneath in spots.

"Gooooood morning!" he sang.

"Morning," replied Xxxxxxx.

"Did you sleep well?" he asked.

Xxxxxxx thought about his soaked bed. All things considered, he *had* slept through the whole night, though he didn't feel incredibly rested.

"I think so," he said, "I was pretty tired."

"Good, good. Any plans for this beautiful summer morning?"

"Breakfast," was Xxxxxxx's stale reply.

"*Yum!* You really must check out ~~cuvit~~ then. Tell ggGggg iiiII sent you. She'll treat you well. I recommend the eggs benedict. Oh, but you *must* try the blueberry pancakes if you're visiting 8ui::v."

Xxxxxxx opened his mouth to thank iiiII for his wordy recommendation, but it turned out he wasn't finished.

"Speaking of visiting 8ui:vv, my daughter is coming into town this morning! She's quite an accomplished filmmaker, you know. Most of it is way over my head, but it's really quite something what that girl can do with a camera! She was just in 7*t*hx* shooting something or other, so she said she would come visit her Pop on the way home. What a good kid, eh?"

"Yeah," said Xxxxxxxx, "That's great. Well, thank you for the breakfast recommendation. Have a great day with your daughter."

"And night!" said iiiII, "she'll be staying the night. Big drive ahead of her still! Oh yes. Two days for sure. I'll never understand why I let my little girl move so far away. 'Oh, but 3—-rr/l is the Mecca of the film industry!' she always says. But what about her poor, old dad out here on his lonesome? Hm? Well, I guess I shouldn't say totally lonesome. I've always got my other daughter, NNNn. But you know how teenagers are. Actually... you would have met her last night! She checked you in. Isn't that right?"

"That's right," said Xxxxxxx, "Did you say 3—-rr/l?"

"Yes! Have you been there? Crazy place. Too crazy for me. But LL loves it. She's always telling me her wild stories about people on the subway. Did you know... one time she caught a man just whizzing in the corner! Just right out in the open! I couldn't believe it when she told me. Oh, and the *smell*, she said it was like gasoline. Burning the nose, you know!"

iiiII glanced at his watch.

"Oh! You must be starving! I'm so sorry to keep you. You know how parents are about their kids. Just the other day I was talking to LL, talking about coming to visit, you know, and she goes 'dad! We've been talking for hours! I've really got to go to sleep!'"

He clutched his belly as he giggled, replaying the memory in his head. Xxxxxxx took his chance to jump in.

"I'm on my way to 3—-rr/l. Do you think there's any chance I could get a ride with your daughter? I'd be happy to pay," he said.

"I suppose that's up to her, isn't it? But between you and me, I think she could use a man with her while she's making these long drives. She says she's fine, you know, but sometimes I get nervous. You seem like a nice enough guy, from what I can tell! You definitely beat her last boyfriend, let me tell you. Don't get me started on *that* guy."

I really wish you wouldn't, thought Xxxxxxx.

"This dummy tells my little girl he wants to get married and have kids, that she needs to settle down and stop travelling so often so she can take care of the house. Oooooh, you should have seen her! She was so red in the face I swore she was going to burst! She goes 'you can't tell me what to do! You don't own me!' and kicks his butt to the curb. Yup, that's my girl!"

"My ears are burning," came a voice from behind Xxxxxxx.

"LL!" shouted iiiII, as he threw his arms straight up above his head and waddled past Xxxxxxx towards the door.

Standing in the entrance was a tall, striking, black-haired woman in an olive-green raincoat, blue jeans, white Converse sneakers, and a two-toned brown and blue baseball cap. She threw her arms up and hugged her dad, who rocked her left and right excitedly. When they separated, he kissed her cheek.

"How was the drive? I've been watching the weather channel all morning to see if that storm was headed your way," said iiiII.

"It was really nice, actually. Clear skies the whole way."

"Wonderful! Wonderful!"

iiiII excitedly turned towards Xxxxxxx.

"This is LL, my daughter!" he said.

I'm never going to get this breakfast, thought Xxxxxxx. His head pulsed in agreement.

"Xxxxxxx. Nice to meet you," he said.

She smiled at him and took a step forward to extend an open hand in his direction. He shook it and his heart raced. Standing in the doorway she had been striking, but up close she was drop-dead gorgeous. His mouth went dry as he fumbled for something to say. For the first time since meeting iiiII, Xxxxxxx was grateful for his aversion to silence.

"Xxxxxxx here says he's heading to 3—-rr/l and needs a ride! I don't want to speak for you, but I've been chatting with the fella all morning and he seems like a good guy. Not like kK!"

LL laughed at the reference to her ex. She looked at Xxxxxxx for a moment. He fidgeted uncomfortably, unsure where to put his hands.

"I leave at three. Don't be late," she said.

iiiII looked shocked.

"Three?!" he exclaimed, "I thought you were staying the night! I have a room set aside for you!"

"I know, I'm so sorry dad. I got my dates all mixed up. I have to get this gear back by Thursday, not Friday. If I'm going to make it in time, I can't stay the night."

"I'll pay your late fees!" iiiII exclaimed.

She laughed.

"They're not late fees, dad. Someone else rented the gear, so I need to get it back to the office for them. I can't stay, I'm sorry."

iiiII pouted for a moment before springing back into his usual, jovial self. If he only had the afternoon with his daughter, he wasn't going to spend it moping!

From behind them, the motel door opened and Xxxxxxx recognized the bad-tempered teenager from the night before. Her sister and father gave her an enthusiastic welcome, which she shrugged off apathetically. She sat behind the desk and began reading her book.

"Well then I guess we should be off! Your sister and I are going to grab something to eat, NNNn. We'll be back later!" called iiiII.

"Nice to meet you," said Xxxxxxx weakly.

LL looked back at him over her shoulder and pointed in his direction.

"Three p.m.," she said.

"Three p.m.," repeated Xxxxxxx.

They left and Xxxxxxx followed them out, making sure to walk in the opposite direction. He had never gotten directions to ~~cuvit~~, but if that was iiiII's recommendation, it was likely also where they were headed, and Xxxxxxx didn't feel like bumping into them at the same restaurant. He'd had enough conversation for a while.

He came across another restaurant advertising blueberry pancakes in the window and stepped in.

CHAPTER TWENTY

M woke up to a sudden bright light. Her eyes melted out of their sockets and her head pounded. She gasped sharply.

The office supply store employee shrieked and dropped the lid to the dumpster, immersing M back into darkness. The lid clattered down deafeningly, and her head pounded once more.

She could hear the employee outside, attempting to talk themselves through finding a living human being somewhere there never should have been one. Finally, they steeled themselves, took three deep breaths, and opened the lid again. Light poured in once more, and M sucked air back through bared teeth as she squeezed her eyes closed. When she gained the courage to open them, she found herself face-to-face with a young boy, surely no older than seventeen.

"Boo!" she said.

The boy tensed, ready to flee, but stood his ground.

"What're you doing?" he asked shakily.

"Trying to find a way out of this situation," replied M.

Not the answer he was expecting, his brow furrowed as his brain attempted to catch up with the conversation, factoring in this new information. When it did, he was sufficiently disarmed to allow a small chuckle to escape his lips.

M put her hand out.

"You going to help me out of here, or what?"

The young boy wasn't sure what the protocol was for finding a living woman in the dumpster, but he knew he didn't want to be rude, so he grabbed M's hand and helped her down.

"Thanks," said M, and she began to walk away.

"Wait!" called the boy.

M stopped and turned.

"What?"

The boy thought about it for a moment. He wasn't sure "what." A few seconds passed before M turned again and walked away. The boy watched as she made her way to the end of the alley and turned the corner back to the street.

Once there, M continued down the main road in the opposite direction of the park she had sat in the night before. Soon she came upon a diner serving breakfast.

"Table for one, please" she said.

The hostess hesitated, noticeably uncomfortable. Seeing where this was going, M pulled the twenty out of her pocket.

"I have money. I'm not homeless, just dirty," she said.

The hostess turned a bright red and began backpedaling for a misstep she had never taken, in the process accidentally revealing how spot on M's supposition had been. Eventually she calmed herself, apologized, and guided M to a table.

M could feel the stares of the other patrons in the diner. Some would steal glances whenever she looked away, others would boldly lock eyes with her if their gazes crossed paths, only to turn away after M pulled a face, knocking them out of their trance. She took their reactions as a sign that she was far from any large city. The sea of only white faces was a strong second clue.

She refused to let the gawking customers bother her and ordered the largest platter she could get for under twenty dollars. She was going to enjoy this breakfast, whether she felt like a zoo animal or not.

The food came and she ate ravenously. At one point the manager came over to kindly ask if she could keep her sounds of enjoyment down, as it was scaring some of the other clientele. She answered with a thumb up, her face busy tearing through a pancake.

"I like your style," said another voice.

M looked up. Sitting at the table directly across from her was a fifty-something-year-old man with shoulder-length brown hair and beard to match, both speckled with grey. He wore an old burgundy button-down shirt that looked about to burst around his pot belly. The rest of him was hidden behind the table.

"Fanks," said M through a mouthful of food.

"You travelin'?" he asked.

M swallowed before answering this time.

"What tipped you off?"

The man laughed.

"I've got a sense for these things. Where ya headed?"

"3—-rr/l," said M.

"3—-rr/l, eh? Big drive! You haulin' too?"

M figured he must be a freight trucker. She supposed that was just about the only kind of visitor a town like that usually got.

"No," said M, "I'm the cargo these days."

"Hitchin'? Lord! You're tougher'n you look," he said.

M took that as a compliment.

"Tell you what. I'm headin' west, but the four-oh-nine doesn't split till just after 5rt-#. I could take you that far if you want. 3—-rr/l should just be a few hours northeast after that."

M couldn't believe her luck. She thanked the trucker profusely and he moved his meal over to her table to join her. They didn't speak much but sat together until they both finished and paid for their respective bills. M left a small tip, leaving her with just under five dollars from her original twenty. God bless small town breakfasts.

• • • •

The ride was generally uneventful. The trucker would periodically burst into song if he recognized a tune on the radio, but otherwise the pair kept to themselves. It wasn't until the sun began to set that the trucker spoke. They were approaching a truck stop.

"I'm gonna pop in for a coffee. Figure we might as well keep goin' if that's okay with you."

"I'm not driving," shrugged M.

"Okay then. Want anything?"

M's hand flew to her flask in her jacket pocket.

"Could you get me a big jug of water?" she asked.

"You bet."

When the trucker returned, he passed M a two-litre bottle of water. She threw her head back and began guzzling it as he put on his seatbelt. When she had to stop or else risk drowning herself, she asked how much she owed him. He brushed it off, saying it was on him.

M eventually fell asleep and slept better than she had all week. When she woke up, the truck was parked. She stretched as far as the cabin would allow and rolled out a kink in her neck. The trucker was gone.

She unbuckled her seatbelt and crawled out of the truck with her duffel bag, just in case. She was at another truck stop. She began to look around for some indication of what town she was in when the trucker came bounding up to her from across the dirt lot.

"Oh good, you're up," he said, "I've gotta hit the road again. You got all your stuff?"

Putting two and two together, M realized she must be in 5rt-#. She held up her bag. The trucker laughed and shook his head.

"I wish you all the luck in the world, lady" he said.

"My name's M," said M.

The trucker smiled and stuck his hand out.

"Z."

"No shit!" exclaimed M.

"No shit," laughed Z.

The pair shook hands.

"It was very nice to meet you, Z. Thank you for taking me so far. You have no idea how much it means to me."

"You're alright, kid," said Z. He pat M heartily on the shoulder with a smile, then walked off behind her back towards the truck.

M's head throbbed. She reached for her flask but paused halfway. Right across the lot was a coffee shop called ~~ort~~. An idea popped into her head. She suddenly heard Xxxxxxx's voice in her head say, *the breakfast of champions.*

"Oatmeal's for suckers," she said to herself.

She walked into ~~ort~~ and ordered a bagel with cream cheese and a small black coffee. The cashier smiled a crooked grin at her. Again, she flashed back to ~~mins~~, when she had first seen

Ddd, Xxxxxx's coworker, suck her rotten teeth at them both. This man's teeth looked like they were seconds from falling out, and M caught herself counting them every time he opened his mouth to see if he had lost any since the time before that. What was it about these rural 0() towns and poor dental hygiene? Of course, the only conclusive answer she got was that placing bets on tooth decay doesn't make you a lot of friends, and she was eventually asked to leave.

Her stomach grumbled.

"I know, old girl. We'll get you something soon," she cooed.

Her coffee dreams dashed, M took a nip of whiskey to soothe her growing headache. The sun was high, and the bright summer sun was harsh on her eyes, especially reflecting off the hoods of lines of parked eighteen-wheelers.

She peeled off her leather jacket and tossed it over her shoulder, considering her next steps. She was so close to 3—-rr/l, she could taste it. She spotted a line of dumpsters on the side of ~~ort~~ near the loading dock. She bet one of those was dedicated to paper and cardboard recycling. If she could get her hands on a marker, she could fashion a sign and set up near the gas station. Then all she'd have to do is wait until the right person came along and bingo, she'd be on her way.

She laughed at her own naiveté, but headed towards the dumpsters nonetheless.

Sounds like one of Xxxxxx's ideas, she thought.

It struck her how often she had been thinking of Xxxxxx since she left 0xx-M-. That funny looking man from a part of her life she hoped would eventually become a footnote, if not discarded entirely. She wondered what he might be up to, now that she was outside of 9(a.

She felt a pang of guilt in her chest.

"Fuck," she said out loud, kicking the dirt with her boot. A tan cloud flew up from the earth and soared into the sky, carried away by the breeze.

0xx-M- was supposed to be a quick stop on her way to 3—-rr/l, no more significant than 5rt-#, or any of these godforsaken towns she had already forgotten the names of. Meeting Xxxxxxx made things inconvenient.

She took a large swig of whiskey. Tears welled in her eyes from the vapors. She swallowed quickly and fell into a coughing fit. Her head swam. She stumbled. With nothing to hold on to she swayed left and right, walking in long arcs until she finally reached the building. She rested against it with her eyes closed. The sun beat down heavily on her head, and she wiped sweat from her brow. Clarity returned slowly.

It turned out her intuition was spot on, and she not only found cardboard, but a stack of unused promotional tray liners in one of the dumpsters. They were printed single-sided, so M grabbed a few to doodle on while she waited for a ride.

The gas station attendant was happy to lend M a marker for her sign, and even offered to mention her to anyone headed northeast. She thanked him, despite the redundant offer, as she set up outside the only door to the building.

While she waited for someone to arrive, she swapped out her doodle idea for another. She would write Xxxxxxx a letter to explain where she was. She owed him at least that much. She put the marker to the page and wrote in comically large handwriting to her favourite cashier. She ended up filling all three pages, her writing getting smaller and tighter at the bottom of each page as she struggled to fit in everything she wanted to say while using a tool that made her writing look like a preschooler's.

Finished, it dawned on her that she had no idea where to send it. Her phone was a doorstop at this point, and she never got Xxxxxxx's address. She contemplated for a minute if she could send it to ~~mins~~ somehow before giving up and stuffing it in her duffel bag.

Her stomach grumbled again, so she went back inside the gas station and bought herself a bottle of water and a bag of pretzels with the last of her cash. She would've killed for some fruits or veggies.

Out front she found another trucker standing by her sign.

"This yours?" he asked.

"Depends. Which way you headed?" she retorted.

"4-/^f-#. I can take you to 3—-rr/l no problem."

"I don't have any cash," said M.

His eyes darted down to the food in her hands, then back up to meet hers. He raised one eyebrow.

"...Anymore," she finished.

He smirked.

"I don't mind. You look like you've had some shit luck. Consider me your lucky ghost."

Now it was M's turn to smirk, mostly at the phrase "lucky ghost."

"Well, hello, mister Ghost. I think I'll take you up on that."

"Alrighty then. Just have to pay and I'll be right out," he said, starting for the door.

M thrust the marker at him.

"Mind giving this back to the cashier inside?"

The trucker snorted and took the marker without another word.

CHAPTER TWENTY-ONE

Xxxxxx looked over at the clock on the wall of the motel lobby. 3:17pm.

Don't be late, he mocked internally.

As if she had been waiting for her cue, LL walked through the front door. Her dad wasn't with her. Xxxxxxx guessed they must have said their goodbyes already, and his theory gained validity as he noticed a faint redness around her eyes.

"Ready?" she asked.

Xxxxxxx nodded and grabbed his pile of belongings.

LL ran over to give NNNn a hug, which she protested to loudly, before returning to follow Xxxxxxx out of the building.

Parked out front was an ice blue Mini Cooper stuffed full of black metal stands, cables, sandbags, camera bags, and lighting gear.

"Glad you packed light," said LL as she breezed past him towards the car.

Xxxxxxx watched her ass bounce back and forth with every step and his heart rate quickened. The front of his jeans tightened. He took a deep breath.

Cool it, he thought, *this is going to be a long drive. Don't embarrass yourself too early.*

He shook it off and followed her to the car.

She got in the driver's side and pulled on her seatbelt. After starting the engine, she did a quick shoulder check and pulled out onto the road.

"Alright, Xxxxxxx, was it? If you're riding in my car, you've got to tell me a little something about yourself. I don't give rides to strangers," she said, all the while adjusting her mirrors.

Xxxxxxx fidgeted in his seat. This was his chance, finally, to redefine himself. He had been thinking about how he wanted to answer this question all afternoon. He turned the phrase over in his head a few times, steeling himself.

"I'm a poet," he said.

His insides withered. Every organ turned to dust. He felt like such a fool. A walking cliché. A fake. A phony.

"Oh, cool! Any particular style?" she asked.

Xxxxxxx blinked. That hadn't been the reaction he was expecting. He had expected laughter, maybe a scoff. Or, if not blatantly hostile, at least a swift change of subject.

"Anybody home?" asked LL.

Xxxxxxx snapped back to the present.

"Uh, yeah. Free verse," he replied.

"My favourite. I've got a friend back home who just published her second book of free verse poetry. Are you published?"

Xxxxxxx's mouth went dry. Suddenly he wanted nothing more than to jump out of the moving vehicle. On the highway now, his conviction remained. Imposter syndrome played him like a fiddle, and his confidence waned considerably.

"I... no, I... uh," he stammered.

"Ah, that's alright. In time. You definitely made the right choice coming to 3—-rr/l, though. Arts capital of 0()! If you're any good, someone will find you," encouraged LL, "Is that why you're moving?"

Xxxxxxx considered correcting her that he wasn't moving to 3—-rr/l, just visiting, but realized that to do so might lead to him to reveal his entire plan was dictated by a brochure he had found in a hotel lobby. Instead, he said, "something like that," hoping she would move on.

"That's great. I'd be happy to put you in touch with some friends of mine when we reach the city, if you'd like," she said.

"That would be incredible!" said Xxxxxxx.

"Done deal. What part of town are you staying in?"

"I uh, well... I was kind of just going to figure that out when I got there," he said.

Her eyes went wide.

"You're just walking into 3—-rr/l expecting to find a place to stay just like that?" she asked, snapping her fingers on the word "that."

"Kinda, yeah," he said.

LL snorted.

"I'm sorry. That's rude of me. At least tell me you've got a job lined up."

Xxxxxxx blushed.

"No!" she yelled, before throwing her head back in laughter.

Xxxxxxx looked out the window down at the road as it whizzed by. He weighed whether the sting of the pavement would hurt more or less than the embarrassment he was feeling right there in that Mini Cooper. When LL collected herself, she apologized again.

"I'll tell you what. Whenever we stop next, I'll give my roommate a call. If she doesn't mind, you can crash on our couch for a few days while you look for work."

"I... thank you!" blurted Xxxxxxx.

"Yeah, yeah. I can't leave you out on the street like that. 3—-rr/l gets really busy over the summer. With all the tourists, you're not likely to find a hotel in the city that's not at capacity for another month or two, tops. Same goes for motels, hostels, AirBnBs, you name it."

"Fuck. Thank you so much."

Xxxxxxx slumped back in his seat. He hated that this kept happening to him. It seemed no matter how he tried to prepare, the universe was there to throw a new detail at him he hadn't considered. He looked over at the angel in the driver's seat and his brain flooded with oxytocin.

"Your dad mentioned you were a filmmaker," said Xxxxxxx.

She laughed musically.

"Did he, now?"

"Yeah. Said you were 'quite accomplished.'"

She rolled her eyes.

"Whatever *that* means. I've put out a few short films, but none of them have gone very far. He's just a proud dad, is all," she said.

"What're your films about?"

"People!" she beamed, "Always people."

"Why's that?" asked Xxxxxxx.

"You've heard of the Holocene, right?"

He hadn't.

"It's what scientists call the period in which life can be supported on Earth. Where temperatures are predictable, don't fluctuate much, and allow for life as we know it to exist" she said.

"So, like, right now?"

"See, that's the thing! Because humans have evolved so quickly over our existence as a species, we've actually changed the world enough that scientists now say we've entered a new era, the Anthropocene, where human activity is the driving force in the planet's climate."

"So, you make films about people changing the planet?" he asked, aware of how dumb he sounded.

Xxxxxxx's brain hurt. He still had that dull headache he had woken up with and trying to keep up with LL would have been a task on a good day. She was smart, Xxxxxxx realized. Smarter than he was. He felt a smidge narcissistic thinking it, but he had become so used to being the "smart one" back in 0xx-M- that he hadn't considered what it would be like to be on the other end.

"No, silly. That's just an example of how unusual people are. My films are usually a little more sociological," she explained, "I was just in 7*t*hx* shooting one centered around the wage gap."

Xxxxxxx didn't know what the wage gap was either but didn't want to appear any more uneducated than he already did, so he said "oh, I see," and absentmindedly began running his fingertips perpendicular to the pages in the notebook on his lap. They made a flapping noise that drew LL's attention.

"Those your poems?" she asked.

Xxxxxxx tucked the notebook further under his clothes.

"Yeah," he said.

"Would you read me one?"

"There's only two of them, maybe one. I'm not sure. They're not really done."

"Are you having trouble with them?"

Xxxxxx told her all about the poem he had written on his first night, and how it had been destroyed after his accident.

"Oh my *god!*" she exclaimed, "that's *awful!* This happened yesterday?!"

Xxxxxx nodded, pulled his hair back around the cut on the top of his head.

"Wow. Just wow," she said. She stared ahead out the window. Xxxxxx could see her wheels turning.

After a minute or two, Xxxxxx realized she wasn't going to say anything and decided he would try to write. He attempted another rewrite of his first poem, adding a line about the Anthropocene, but eventually hit the same wall he always hit. He grumbled and shut his notebook.

"What's giving you trouble?" she asked.

"I don't know," said Xxxxxx, "I just can't get it out right."

"Can I offer some advice?"

"Shoot."

"Whenever I feel myself getting stuck a creative rut, I change perspective. Take a look from another character's eyes. There might be a piece of the same story that suddenly looks entirely different."

Xxxxxx thought about how he had done this already every time he had learned something new about M. How the story, and the light in which M was cast, had shifted just like LL was saying. He thought about how to apply that concept to his poem.

Suddenly, the memory of TtttT asking if porn stars got paid six figure salaries jumped into his head, and he burst out laughing.

"That sounds promising," said LL.

"Just remembering the tow truck driver that picked me up. Funny guy."

"Why don't you let him write your poem?"

"Excuse me?" said Xxxxxxx.

"Write it from his point of view. It doesn't have to be the final draft or anything, just get those juices flowing!"

Xxxxxxx could hear the passion in her voice. She wasn't just trying to give him advice, she was cheering him on. He felt butterflies in his stomach and his face reddened. He had always felt exempt from, maybe even above, the physiological responses of attraction, finding them embarrassing, but talking with LL made him feel like a twelve-year-old boy in a poorly written teen drama, all blushing cheeks and stinky pits. Hearing LL's voice tremble with excitement not from creating something, but from the *idea* of creating something struck Xxxxxxx as incredible.

He grabbed his pen and began writing again, this time imagining he was TtttT.

Sitting in my truck

Thinkin bout porn stars

Xxxxxxx laughed and scratched it all out.

"You can do this!" cheered on LL.

"Okay, thanks," said Xxxxxxx. His mind boggled at how quickly her words of encouragement had gone from encouraging to irritating.

He wasn't sure how to start. TtttT had been such a bright, kind-hearted man. Imagining him sitting in a hotel room high out of his mind talking to inanimate objects just didn't strike Xxxxxxx as something he would do.

That's when he remembered the mother and daughter from his first night. He had written a line about no movie star being able to hold a light to his customer service smile, or something like that. The details didn't matter. What mattered was that he had found his answer. What if TtttT, with all his outward joy and happiness, had been wearing his own customer service smile? What if he was just as miserable as Xxxxxx had been back in 0xx-M-, and Xxxxxx just hadn't been able to recognize it?

He imagined TtttT sitting in a dimly lit trailer, one lamp in the corner, sitting on a torn-up couch surrounded by dirty dishes, trash, and old nudie mags. What a thought. He put his pen to paper.

Sitting on the couch
High as a skyscraper
Playboys and dishes litter the table
The girl on the TV screen
She's on top of the world
She gets paid in six figures
To choke on his cock
While he pulls on her curls
There's no movie star that can hold a light to me
When I put a smile on everyday

"Hey," said Xxxxxx to himself, "what do you know?"

"How's it going over there?" asked LL.

"I... good, I think!" said Xxxxxx.

He felt emboldened by LL's exercise. He continued writing, forging forward and cutting back continuously over the next hour until he had filled all the space in the notebook that wasn't water damaged.

"Uh oh," said Xxxxxxx.

"What's up?"

"I'm out of paper."

"Uh oh."

"That's what I said."

"I think there's a rest stop coming up soon. Want to grab a nice 0()-themed pad and pen?" she laughed.

"Oh, you bet," said Xxxxxxx sarcastically. Then he thought about it.

"Actually, well... maybe, yeah," he stuttered.

LL laughed again.

Ten minutes later they came to the rest stop. Xxxxxxx bee-lined for the souvenir shop and grabbed the first notebook he could find. It wasn't until the cashier picked it up to scan it that Xxxxxxx realized the cover was a hologram of the 0() flag blowing to and fro in the wind. The cashier had barely finished asking Xxxxxxx if he would like a bag before the word "yes" flew from his lips.

He bought himself a burger and met LL in front of the building. She was smoking a cigarette and appeared to be otherwise empty handed.

"Not hungry?" asked Xxxxxxx.

She exhaled.

"Places like this never have any vegan options, so it's just me and Ciggy Tardust over here," she said, lifting her cigarette.

"Wham, bam, thank you ma'am," said Xxxxxxx.

"We should be about an hour from 3'\\]. I know a good vegan place there we can stop into," she said.

She took another drag from her cigarette. Xxxxxxx's head throbbed.

"Do you think I'd be able to get any weed there?" he asked.

"The restaurant or the town?"

"I'm not picky," said Xxxxxxx.

"I'm not sure, sorry. I wish I'd known you were looking! I could have hooked you up with my old guy in 8ui::v."

Xxxxxxx didn't see how that helped him but thanked her for the offer anyway.

LL ashed her cigarette and nodded at the bag in Xxxxxxx's hands.

"Got your notebook?"

"Yup," said Xxxxxxx.

"Let me see," she smiled.

Xxxxxxx blushed.

"No," he said.

LL grabbed for the notebook. Xxxxxxx tried to snatch it back, but only caught the corner of the bag, stretching it until the notebook popped out and into LL's arms. She tossed her head back, laughing.

"YES!" she exclaimed, "This is amazing. Great choice on the holograph!"

"Bite me," said Xxxxxxx with a smile.

CHAPTER TWENTY-TWO

It was an hour down the road when smoke started billowing out of the front of the Lucky Ghost's Peterbilt.

"Shit, fuck, goddamnit," he cursed.

He pulled over, popped the hood, and he and M disembarked. He waved back black clouds of smoke with his right arm, his left wrapped around his mouth and nose. When the clouds subsided, he took one look at the engine and threw both hands up in the air.

"GODDAMNIT, I TOLD THEM! I *TOLD* THEM!"

He raged for a few minutes longer before stopping to catch his breath. M did her best to stay out of his way, moving further down the road. When he saw this, he apologized for frightening her and informed her they were stuck until he could get a tow truck out to pick them up.

"How long do you think that'll be?" M asked.

"Well, the closest town is 5rt-#, an hour back. I guess there's your answer," he muttered. He was still in a justifiably foul mood from what seemed like an avoidable malfunction.

M didn't like the sound of that. She knew if she went back to 5rt-# she would have to spend another night, and more than anything she wanted to keep moving forward. She thanked the ironically named Lucky Ghost one more time and walked down the road to try and flag down another ride.

. . . .

After a few more hours of walking, the sun was beginning to take a toll on her. She was burnt, drunk, hungry, and severely dehydrated. She was about to give up and pass out in the ditch when a bright green Corolla slowed down and pulled up next to her. The passenger-side window rolled down to reveal a young blonde who couldn't have been older than twenty-one. Her hair was tied in pigtails, and her face was heavily made up in bright neon shades of pink and blue.

"Hey babe! Need a ride?" she smacked through a wad of gum the size of a ping pong ball.

Exhausted, M nodded and said, "thank you."

The girls chattered amongst each other, rearranging themselves in the backseat to accommodate one more passenger. There turned out to be four of them – two up front, two in the back – and each dressed in colours as garish as the last. The blonde stuck her head out the window.

"Of course, babe! Get in!" she said.

The girls spent the rest of the ride fawning over M. Over her eye, over her sunburns, over her dirty clothing, over her bravery for travelling alone. M could hardly stand it.

They offered to drive her as far as she needed them to. They were on a road trip and claimed to welcome detours. When she told them she was headed for 3—-rr/l, they all howled it together like wolves in heat.

"3333333————————rrrrrrr///////lllllllll!"

After the novelty of M's existence wore off and the women lost interest, she fell asleep against the window of the car. When she awoke, she was alone, and the car was parked. She heard muffled voices coming from outside.

She sat up and rubbed her face. There was a kink in her neck.

"She's up!" she heard someone say.

M crawled out from the Corolla and onto the sidewalk. They were parked on the street in front of a tall, old building with ornate metal fencing around the perimeter of the property. At the sight of M, the young women became a frenzy of enthusiastic "good mornings" and "did you sleep wells." She did her best to answer everyone individually, when the blonde, still smacking the same wad of gum, spoke up above them all.

"We wanted to do something special to help you out, so we all, like, pitched in together and got you a hotel for the night!"

She handed M a hotel room key card.

Overwhelmed by the gesture, M grabbed the women and pulled them in for a group hug. They simultaneously tilted their noses away from her, but squeezed tight, nonetheless.

"How can I repay you?" asked M.

"Don't worry about it, babe! Girls have to have each other's backs!" squeaked the blonde.

M smiled. In another lifetime she might have had a well-crafted response ready to go, but the sheer generosity of the gesture proved too much for her to be anything but thankful. They all said their goodbyes, and M watched them drive off down the street and around the corner, pop radio blaring. Saints in neon pumps.

A few properties down from where M was standing, the street intersected with another. On the corner was a sign that told her she was at the intersection of 2nd and Main. Above the street names was a city logo M had only ever seen in photographs.

"3—-rr/l," she said out loud.

She said it again, and again, enjoying the sound of the word, when she was bumped out of the way.

"Watch where you're going!" snapped a short, middle-aged man as he walked past.

M snapped out of her reverie. The streets were full of pedestrians of all shapes, sizes, and temperaments. It had been almost a month since she had found herself in a city remotely close to the size of 3—-rr/l, and with all she had been through she had almost completely forgotten what it felt like. The street buzzed with energy. Cars, trucks, bikes, rollerblades, skateboards, and electric scooters whizzed past, each adding its own distinct sound to the cacophony of the city. Skyscrapers towered overhead, and advertisements covered every surface they could be squeezed onto.

She took a deep breath and fell into a coughing fit. Between the stench of air pollution and her own body odour, the air around her made her feel as if she was a walking biohazard. She checked the room number on her key card and went straight there to wash up.

Her room was nicely furnished. Besides the standard desk-TV-twin bed combination, there was a high-backed armchair in the corner with a small table and reading lamp, as well as a small kitchenette.

She stripped in the hallway and stepped into the shower. She turned the valve and gasped as freezing cold water hit her skin but didn't move to escape it. Instead, she closed her eyes and tuned herself in to the water, feeling it heat up slowly until it was a comfortable temperature, and then a bit too hot.

All at once, everything she had been holding in since vV's death, from telling him to take the bus instead of the Chevelle, to leaving Pp behind, to ditching Xxxxxxx without warning back in 0xx-M-, came pouring out of her. She fell to her knees, then on all fours, then to the fetal position, hair tangled uncomfortably around her face. She sobbed uncontrollably, the force of her grief so strong that she felt stuck in place, silently gasping for air with each muscle contraction in her gut. She vomited all over the shower floor and noticed a small amount of blood wash away with half-digested pretzels. Her head throbbed in agony but wouldn't allow her the luxury of passing out, as if her body was finally putting its foot down. It was time to process her grief, whether she was ready or not. She vomited again, this time mostly water. Her stomach ached with the strength of her convulsions. She begged whatever god would listen for mercy, but none came. Minutes passed like hours, and hours like days, painfully wonderful memories of vV flooding back one at a time, until she finally, gratefully, passed out from fatigue.

When she woke up, the shower was still running. The water was still warm, so she figured she couldn't have been out for too long. She reached up and pulled the valve shut. Her skull throbbed, so she moved slowly. Step-by-agonizing-step, M pulled herself out of the shower and onto the toilet seat. She put her head in her hands. She missed vV so much. She missed the way he smelled. The way he would look at her whenever she got him with a particularly good one. The way his body felt against hers. She had no idea how she was going to continue without him. The last month had been nothing short of a nightmare, and she wanted nothing more than to wake up from it and find herself lying in bed with vV as he giggled at Pp passing gas in his sleep, just like it had always been.

She stood and looked at herself in the mirror. She barely recognized her reflection. Bruised, burned, battered, the woman looking back at her looked tough. But she didn't feel tough. In fact, she had never felt weaker.

She wished Xxxxxxx was there. More than ever, she needed a friend.

Before she had left 0xx-M-, M had had the foresight to write Xxxxxxx's number down on the inside tag of her duffel bag. vV's family was the only family she had left, and she thought it counterproductive to reach out for help from the very people she had run away from. So, by default, Xxxxxxx had become her emergency contact.

She rang the number on the hotel phone before she had time to think about what to say. She turned a few ideas over in her head as the phone rang, and rang, and rang.

Would it kill you to get voicemail? she thought.

She hung up, making a mental note to try again later. In the meantime, she still needed to come up with a plan. She wasn't out of the woods yet. This hotel was only good for the night, which meant she needed to find income immediately or be back on the street.

She was pretty sure she had a copy of her resume up in the cloud somewhere, so all she needed was internet access and some change to print a few and she would be good to go.

That's enough for tonight, she thought. She was spent and deserved a night off. Just one. And maybe a nip of whiskey to celebrate.

She dumped back her flask and swallowed the last of her supply.

• • • •

"What do you *mean* incorrect password?" said M, giving the printer a hearty smack.

She was tired, and irritable. Without any whiskey left she had slept horribly, tossing and turning all night. The hot, crowded streets made moving quickly difficult, and M had already taken the heads off two people just on her trip down the block to the print shop.

An employee risked making it three when he approached the grumpy M, asking if there was anything he could do to be of service.

"Yeah, wanna give me a job?" she replied.

"Not if that's your idea of tech support," said the employee.

Too annoyed to appreciate the joke, M scoffed and tried her password again. It was the only password she had for anything. It *had* to work. When the red X reappeared at the top of the screen, M cursed loudly.

"Hey! Cool it," said the employee.

"Listen, man, unless you know why this piece of junk isn't accepting my password can you just leave me alone?"

The employee stood there, unmoving.

"Well?" said M.

"I know why this piece of junk isn't accepting your password," he said, and smiled.

He excused himself and reached down towards the keyboard. He selected the password field, deleted everything in it, and began hammering on the "P" key. Nothing happened onscreen. He looked over at M, who was practically nose-to-nose with him from sharing the same tiny screen, and raised his eyebrows.

"Okay, what now?" said M impatiently.

"Follow me. You can log on using the staff computer right over there, and it'll print right here."

She did as she was told, paid the man, and soon had a small stack of resumes ready to be delivered across town.

She had spent that morning panhandling for change. 3—-rr/l was so densely populated and had such a large community of unhoused people that those with money to spare had become conditioned to their existence. They barely glanced at M when she stuck a paper cup out at them, instead dropping in whatever change they had and scuttling away before they had to interact with her.

As the employee returned her change and receipt, he hesitated.

"Hey, I know you're probably not in the mood to hear it, but I'll be kicking myself all day if I don't ask you for your number," he said.

M paused and looked him up and down. He was wearing a rather unflattering grey, white, and red store uniform, but was otherwise quite handsome. His nametag read "AaA."

"You're right, AaA," she said, "I'm not in the mood to hear it."

She grabbed her receipt, change, and stack of resumes and walked out the door.

She prioritized coffeeshops and fast-food chains; anywhere with a high turnover rate that might be expecting a quick start. She also knew that ripped, black jeans and a white t-shirt weren't the most professional attire, so she kept her options realistic.

Eventually, she came across another ~~off~~. She recognized the logo from from the location she had been kicked out of earlier that week. M figured this time couldn't possibly go any worse, so she strode in the front door confidently.

CHAPTER TWENTY-THREE

3'\\] turned out to be much more than an hour down the road. When the clock hit the second hour, neither of them were speaking anymore. LL was too tired to hold up a conversation. Xxxxxxx offered to drive on a few occasions, but every time he did, she would insist 3'\\] was right around the next bend.

Finally, like a flashing neon sign that read "YOU'RE SAVED," they passed the 3'\\] city limits. There was a palpable sense of relief in the air, which was soon met with the smell of fast food being pumped out into the street to entice passing travelers.

As if reading his mind, LL said, "I feel like a cartoon floating through the air after a freshly baked pie," and Xxxxxxx knew exactly what she meant. Despite having eaten a burger at their last stop, he was ready for more.

They pulled into the parking lot of a restaurant called ~~vindi~~. The outside was painted a bright white with green detailing, potted plants hanging from every surface that would support them, and paintings of plants on every surface that wouldn't.

"This the place?" asked Xxxxxxx.

"Subtle, right?" said LL.

They both got the largest bowls on the menu and scarfed them down in minutes. Satisfied, they sat back in their chairs with their bellies hanging out. LL burped.

"Whoo! Sorry!"

They both laughed.

"I don't know about you, but I'm beat. What do you say we crash here for the night?" said LL.

"The town or the restaurant?" joked Xxxxxxx.

"I'm not picky," she replied.

She winked at him and pretended to fall asleep, snoring loudly. The waiter passed by with the bill, and, after a short repose, LL quickly snapped back into her sleeping bit. Xxxxxxx thought it cute, but was unsure how to explain to her that he couldn't afford to pay for them both.

Before he could say anything, she sat up and flashed a credit card at the waiter, who pulled a debit machine from his apron.

"You're not—" started Xxxxxxx.

"I am," said LL, "It's my fault we stopped here, so I'm covering it."

Xxxxxxx wanted to argue with her that there was no reason she should pay for his full meal but knew his bank account could use a break, so he said thank you and shut his mouth before anything else came out.

Outside the restaurant, LL led the way to the car. She spun on her heels to meet Xxxxxxx's eyes, which snapped back up to her face. She walked backwards across the parking lot as she spoke.

"So, which way should we go, do you think?"

Xxxxxxx thought about it for a minute, his brow furrowed.

"There's no wrong answer," assured LL.

"Hm?"

"You look very concerned. There's no wrong answer, just asking for your opinion."

Xxxxxxx laughed.

"I was just weighing my options," he said.

She furrowed her brow comically and put on a funny voice to mock him, repeating "just weighing my options."

They both laughed.

"Okay, fuck it. Left, then," said Xxxxxxx.

"Ay-ay," replied LL with a salute.

Left ended up bringing them back the way they came, so LL did a U-turn before hitting the city limits and they headed further back into 3'\\]. Shortly down the road they hit a hostel called ~~daxit~~.

LL pulled into the small corner lot and paid the attendant sitting in the booth at the far end. When she returned, they went inside together.

"Hi, welcome to ~~daxit~~!" said the receptionist, a tall, curly-haired man with a smile the size of Xxxxxxx's entire fist.

"Hi," said LL, "What are the chances you've got two private rooms available?"

The receptionist clacked at his keyboard.

"Ooh! You're in luck. We've got *three* private rooms available right now," he said.

"Well, we only need two of 'em!" said LL in a sing-songy tone. Xxxxxxx recognized a customer service voice when he heard one.

The man escorted them upstairs to their rooms. They passed LL's first, on the second floor. She turned the knob to enter, before pausing and turning to look back at Xxxxxxx.

"Lobby at eight?" she asked.

"Sounds good," he replied.

"Night!"

"Night."

The receptionist hadn't stopped with them on the landing, so Xxxxxxx bounded after him, taking the steps two at a time. When he reached the next floor, the receptionist was waiting for him at the open door to his room.

"Voila! Enjoy your stay," he said.

Xxxxxxx thanked him and watched him float away as if he haunted the place rather than ran it.

Xxxxxxx's room was a grey cube with a twin bed in the far-right corner, and a dresser with a small TV and digital clock on it against the wall to his immediate right. To his left was another door that led to a shared bathroom, which Xxxxxxx picked up after reading the word "vacant" in green above the lock mechanism. Straight ahead was a sliding door that opened onto a small balcony. Xxxxxxx went straight for it.

The sun was starting to set now. He wished he could enjoy it, but his headache was really starting to get to him. He looked down at the people on the street below, hoping someone might be carrying a sign that said "drug dealer" on it. Perhaps unsurprisingly, he came up short.

He went back inside and lay down in bed. Maybe he could sleep it off.

· · · ·

Hours passed, the sun set, but Xxxxxxx stayed awake.

He stared at the ceiling, replaying the events of the last week in his head over and over. Not with any emotion attached, except possibly for wonder.

He felt almost numb to it all now. What had happened to the exhilarating life of being on the road? The thrill had diminished very quickly under the shadow of real-life consequences and Xxxxxxx was beginning to feel baseless. Had he been wrong this whole time? He couldn't imagine living a life so chaotic for the rest of his days. Maybe "worldview" wasn't quite the goal he expected it would be.

What was it that he wanted then? What was it that M had given him a taste of, that drew him in to her? He felt it in LL as well. A sense of safety, almost. Could that be it? Was he so boring that his life goal was to feel safe?

Clearly not, he thought, remembering the flash of the pickup's headlights in his rearview mirror.

He looked over at the digital clock on the dresser. It read 01:38 in harsh red light. Frustrated, he crawled out of bed and put some clothes on. He remembered seeing a walkway that led behind the building on the way in, with a sign saying something about a hostel garden, so he decided to check it out.

The pathway was well lit, string lights hanging from wooden beams overhead. Hydrangeas lined both sides of a stone pathway that eventually opened into a large courtyard with a massive, diverse garden all around the perimeter. A small fountain and pond stood in the center of the courtyard. Sitting on the edge of the concrete ledge surrounding the pond was LL, smoking another cigarette.

"Hey, you," she said as Xxxxxxx entered the courtyard.

"Can't sleep either?" asked Xxxxxxx.

"Nah," she replied, exhaling smoke.

"You got another one of those?"

She pulled out a pack of Camels and passed him one, along with her lighter. He sat down beside her and lit up. He felt dizzy as the nicotine entered his bloodstream, then relaxed.

"Never got that weed, huh?" asked LL.

He shook his head.

"Sucks. I used to smoke all the time, and when I cut down I would get these nasty withdrawal symptoms. Apparently it's different for everyone, but for me I would have trouble sleeping, and whenever I woke up, I'd have sweat right through my sheets."

"Shit, I think that happened to me last night," said Xxxxxxx.

"I'll hook you up when we get to 3—-rr/l. There's a dispensary right near my place I go to every so often."

"Thank you," said Xxxxxxx as emphatically as he could.

They locked eyes for a moment.

"My pleasure," said LL.

Xxxxxxx's heart raced. He struggled to think of something to say.

"You call your roommate yet?" he asked.

"Hm? Oh, yeah, I did. All good." she replied.

"Oh, good," said Xxxxxxx.

LL's eyes darted down to his mouth, then back up to meet his.

"Good," she repeated.

The word hung in the air for a moment, like the plumes of LL's cigarette. Visible for a moment, then fading away into nothingness as it rose into the atmosphere.

"You're really cute, you know that?" said LL.

Xxxxxxx felt like one of those thumb push puppets after someone had released the tension on his string skeleton. In other words, he went to mush. LL leaned forward, and by the time he realized what was happening, he was kissing her. Hell, she was kissing *him*. He put his hands on her waist and pulled her in tight. His hand slid down to her ass.

"Want to come back to my room?" she asked.

Xxxxxx smiled and said yes, yes, he did.

• • • •

The next morning, LL and Xxxxxx were awoken by LL's smartphone alarm chiming and vibrating as if it were throwing a tantrum. She swung her arm over at it, poking and swiping until the racket stopped, mid-phrase. She sighed heavily and pulled herself up to a sitting position.

"Already?" grumbled Xxxxxx, eyes still closed.

"Yup," sighed LL.

Xxxxxx sat up on the edge of the bed. He had slept well, if not for long. He felt rested. He reached down, retrieved the boxers he'd worn the night before from inside his jeans, and pulled them on.

"How'd you sleep?" asked LL.

"Really well. You?"

"Fantastic."

She winked and pulled her shirt over her head.

When they'd finished dressing, the pair grabbed a couple bagels from the communal kitchen (cream cheese for Xxxxxx, hummus for LL), checked out at the front desk, and got right back on the road. In high spirits, they occupied themselves with road games like seeing how many words they could spell using the letters on passing license plates or casting bets on the colour of the next vehicle to appear around the bend. Xxxxxx's headache remained, but there wasn't much he would be able to do about that until he got into the city.

Not far outside of 3'\\], LL exclaimed, "look! There it is!" and pointed towards the horizon.

Xxxxxxx sat up straight in his seat, at full attention. Just over the hill he could see it; the 3—-rr/l skyline. Tall spires and rectangles of varying widths and heights spanned the length of his vision. He scanned back and forth, looking for the conical turrets of the 3—-rr/l Basilica.

"This is my favourite part about coming home," said LL.

"I can see why," said Xxxxxxx, dumbfounded.

"From here it's so peaceful and quiet, you can really enjoy it for what it is."

"What's that?"

"A feat of humankind."

Xxxxxxx let that sink in for a moment. It was true. From so far away, all there was to see was the beauty in the architecture, the striking emblem of our achievements as a species. It was the trunk of a great tree. It was the unturned stone. Deep down, he still knew it was home to hundreds of thousands, if not millions, of tiny little creatures, defecating and feeding and fucking in their own miniature ecosystem, but from where he sat it was only beautiful and nothing else. He considered trying to write about it, but words escaped him.

They continued down the road, the looming skyline of the gargantuan city growing in size both physically and psychologically with every passing mile, until Xxxxxxx could think of nothing but how goddamn *big* everything was. The buildings, the cars, the signs, even the birds were larger than anything Xxxxxxx had ever seen in 0xx-M-. Finally, they hit the city limits.

"Pull over," said Xxxxxxx.

"What's up?" asked LL.

"Please. Pull over."

LL did as she was told and pulled the Mini Cooper onto the shoulder. Xxxxxx unbuckled his seatbelt and got out of the car. He stood, bewildered, in the shadow of the "Welcome to 3—-rr/l, 8^a, Arts Capital of 0()!" sign. LL watched from the driver's seat as he took one step, then two, then fell to his knees. She got out of the car and ran over to him.

"Xxxxxx! You okay?" she cried.

Xxxxxx laughed, slowly at first, building to full hysteria within seconds. He threw his hands up in the air and screamed "WOOHOO!" at the top of his lungs before breaking down in tears of joy.

LL dropped to her knees beside him, and their eyes met.

"What's going on? You okay?" she asked again.

"So okay," said Xxxxxx.

She hugged him, oblivious to the depth of his joy. He hugged her back, and they stayed that way for a full minute before Xxxxxx pulled back.

"Thank you for bringing me here," he said, "You have no idea what this means to me."

"I'm getting a good picture," she laughed, her eyes watering. The intensity of Xxxxxx's joy was beginning to incite an emotional response in her as well. She got up, extending her hand to Xxxxxx. He took it and she pulled him to his feet.

They both dusted off and got back in the car without saying another word.

"Ready?" asked LL.

"Ready," said Xxxxxx.

But he wasn't. LL pulled back onto the highway and drove into 3—-rr/l. Within minutes, Xxxxxxx's elation deflated like a balloon.

The streets were lined with garbage, and he saw lines of people huddled in sleeping bags along the sidewalk with cardboard signs reading "broke and hungry" or "anything helps." Others dressed in all manners of clothing, some of which Xxxxxxx had never even considered to *be* clothing, walked past those signs without so much as a glance, their bodies angled away from them under the weight of multitudes of shopping bags. Their callousness struck Xxxxxxx as not just unkind, but inhumane. He felt deep down that, had he not met LL, this would have been his fate. An invisible human being in a sea of invisible human beings. Lost forever, barely hanging on.

"Why is everyone just ignoring them?" he asked.

LL shook her head.

"If you were on your deathbed, would you want to visit the morgue?"

The weight of her words fell on Xxxxxxx's chest like an anvil. She went on to explain how wages weren't increasing at the same rate as inflation, and how the city was becoming increasingly divided between the rich and poor. She explained gender, age, and race dynamics. At one point, Xxxxxxx had to ask her to stop speaking because he could no longer keep up with what she was saying and didn't want her to waste her breath.

"Sorry, this is kind of my whole deal at the moment," she laughed.

"No, I'm sorry. I feel like I've been living under a rock my whole life," said Xxxxxxx.

LL pulled off the road onto a slanted driveway that led to an underground parking garage. She flashed her key card and the door folded upwards. She parked in a space with a sign that read "reserved," and she and Xxxxxxx took the elevator up to the main floor.

They crossed the lobby to another elevator, where LL flashed her key card again as she selected the eleventh floor. The elevator jerked upwards.

When they disembarked, LL swiftly navigated a few quick turns through the hallway before coming to a pale-yellow door with the alphanumeric "11E" over the peephole.

"Here we are," she said.

She knocked twice before turning the knob and entering.

"Hello?" she called into the apartment.

"LL?" came a woman's voice.

From the back of a large, open concept living space came a short, stocky woman dressed in a Black Spoon t-shirt and ripped black jeans. Her hair was short and spiked up, bleached white.

"uuuuuuU!" yelled LL, throwing her arms unnecessarily high in the air to hug her five-foot roommate.

"How was 7*t*hx*, girl?" asked uuuuuuU.

"Ups and downs. I'll have to tell you all about it later. I've got to get some gear back to the studio ASAP. I'm just here to drop off the stowaway."

She jerked her thumb back towards Xxxxxxx, and uuuuuuU's eyes went wide.

"Oh shit! I didn't see you there, dude," she said.

Xxxxxxx smiled weakly.

"So, you're the poet LL was telling me about!"

She stuck her hand out at him. When he took it, she grabbed tight and yanked him down to her level. He cursed and pulled his hand back, standing up straight.

"I dunno, girl. He's cute, but I think you overhyped him a smidge," she said, loud enough for LL to hear but never taking her eyes off Xxxxxxx.

"uuuuuuU!" protested LL, "that's enough!"

uuuuuuU winked at Xxxxxxx and turned on her heels to meet her roommate.

"Alright, alright! I'll be nice, I promise."

"You'd better," said LL, pointing a finger at her.

Xxxxxxx laughed at the tableau in front of him. LL towering over uuuuuuU, indignantly standing her ground against LL's wagging finger. LL sighed.

"Okay, I've got to go! I'll be back in an hour or so. Play nice," she said, and ran out the door.

uuuuuuU looked Xxxxxxx up and down, hands on her hips, feet shoulder-width apart. A true power stance. Her eyes narrowed to slits, and Xxxxxxx started seriously questioning whether or not he would have to fight her. Suddenly, she softened and smiled a toothy grin.

"I hear you're a weed man!" she said.

"I am," said Xxxxxxx, still unsure how careful he needed to be.

"Relax, dude. I was just fucking with you. I rolled us a joint already."

She flopped down onto one of two couches pushed together in an "L" shape on Xxxxxxx's left and reached under her coffee table for a decorative tin container, pulling from inside it a fat joint. A choir of angels sang, and a heavenly light fell upon it.

She lit it and took a hit before passing it to Xxxxxxx. He sat down on the couch next to her and took as big a hit as he could, ashing on himself.

"Fuck!" he said through a mouthful of smoke.

He pulled the joint from his lips and began coughing wildly. uuuuuuU cackled loudly.

"I remember *my* first time," she said.

"Clever," said Xxxxxxx in a gravelly voice.

He felt the effects come on immediately and sat back on the couch, drifting off slightly. His headache disappeared. He sighed heavily. uuuuuuU passed him the joint again, but he waved it off. He didn't want to overdo it.

"Would you read me some of your poetry?" asked uuuuuuU, now leaning back into the arm of the chair, head lolled back over the cushion, looking up at the ceiling.

"I don't really do that," said Xxxxxxx.

"Why not?"

"It's a little personal, I guess."

"How can you be a poet if you don't show anyone your poems?" she asked.

"Who you are isn't how you feel, though," came M's voice in his head.

He shivered.

Try as he might to deny it, he knew at heart it was still true. He could talk about being a poet all day, but until he shared that poetry with others, he was Schrödinger's cat. A paradox. A poet to himself and no one else. To be a poet to the world, he would have to share his poetry with the world.

"Fine," he said.

He pulled his notebook out from under his clothes and read her his "perfect underdog" poem. He did his best to hide the tremble in his voice, and uuuuuuU did her best not to notice. When he finished, uuuuuuU clapped enthusiastically.

"That's good shit," she said, "There's an open mic tomorrow night at ~~hog~~, you should come with and read some of your stuff!"

"Tomorrow?" said Xxxxxxx. His head swam. He imagined a crowd of people staring at him as he fumbled his way through his half-written work.

"Yeah, dude. Newbies get a free pint on the house too," she said.

"Well, that's nice. That's about all I can afford," said Xxxxxxx.

uuuuuuU cackled once more.

"That's right! LL told me you didn't have a job lined up."

Xxxxxxx sighed.

"Hey, you know what?" said uuuuuuU, suddenly excited by something.

"What?

Instead of answering, uuuuuuU stuck one finger up in the universal signal for "one minute" and pulled out her smartphone. She quickly navigated her way through it, until she found what she was looking for. She turned the phone towards Xxxxxxx. It was open to a post on a social media app he didn't recognize. The post read:

"107.7FM 7*t*hx* NEVER HEARD OF EM LOOKING FOR BLOG WRITERS. SEND RESUMES TO ssSs AT NHOE@1077.COM."

"What's this?" asked Xxxxxxx.

"A friend of mine in 7*t*hx* needs a blog writer for a new segment they're adding to their show. Have you heard of it? No pun intended."

"Yeah, actually. I used to listen to this show back home all the time."

He couldn't believe the coincidence.

"What's the new segment?" he asked.

"Well, they've been getting a lot of people calling in asking for details on where they can follow up on artists or songs they like. They kinda suck for that, so they want to introduce a blog that'll do little segments on the artists they play."

"Shit, that's a lot of bands," said Xxxxxxx.

"Yeah, dude. Lots of hours. Good pay too."

"How can I apply?" asked Xxxxxxx.

"You got a resume?"

"No. I've only ever had one job. Got it in high school."

uuuuuuU looked at him as if he'd just glitched.

"Where you from?" she asked.

"0xx-M-," said Xxxxxxx.

He felt a strange feeling come over him. He had never referred to 0xx-M- as a place he used to live. It had always just been where he was. He liked it.

"Where's that?" continued uuuuuuU.

"9(a. Three, four days from here."

"No wonder you know Never Heard Of Em. You're practically *in* 7*t*hx*."

"I suppose, relatively speaking," said Xxxxxxx. It wasn't remotely close to the truth, but he was feeling generous.

uuuuuuU got up from the couch. When she came back, she was holding a laptop under her right arm and had a bottle of scotch in her left hand.

"What's all this?" asked Xxxxxxx.

"You don't have a resume. These are resume writing tools. I don't see why you're confused."

Xxxxxxx chuckled and got to work.

CHAPTER TWENTY-FOUR

"How's the job hunt?" asked LL, sliding into the booth next to Xxxxxx and uuuuuuU with three open bottles of beer.

"Not too bad," said Xxxxxx, "got a few replies already. Most places are offering me freelance work, but I think that would be fine. At least for now."

"That's great!" said LL.

"Cheers!" said uuuuuuU.

LL and Xxxxxx took a hearty swig of their beers. uuuuuuU, on the other hand, threw her head back and downed the whole bottle in a single go.

She let out a hearty burp.

"Alright, I'm gonna get another! Scootch!" she said, pushing Xxxxxx out of the way.

As soon as she was gone, Xxxxxx began picking at the label on his beer. He had slept on the couch the previous night, and it had left him feeling a bit strange about where he stood with LL. He wasn't sure if their night together in 3'\\] was meant to be a one-off. He certainly hoped not. The more he got to know her, the less worried he was about who he was supposed to be and how he was supposed to become him. Everything seemed to slow down when they were together. He still wanted to write, but he didn't feel that same nagging itch he once used to to get out and see the world. He still wanted to travel. He still wanted to visit 0()'s greatest skylines. He just wanted to take a lifetime to do it. And while it was still far too early to know for sure, he would have been lying to himself if he'd said he hadn't been picturing that lifetime with LL by his side.

"Up next! Hailing all the way from 0xx-M-, 9(a, give a warm ~~hog~~ welcome to Xxxxxxx!" said the MC.

LL erupted in a loud cheer, applauding in unison with the rest of the bar as Xxxxxxx made his way to the stage.

The blinding spotlight was hot on his skin, but not unpleasant. He shielded his eyes against it and looked out over the sea of diverse faces staring back at him. He took a deep breath and felt a profound calm pass through his body. This stage was his. He felt the eyes of the audience glued to him, this strange, vagabond poet born from a town so small it may as well have been a place of fiction. He was mysterious and brooding and could feel the intensity in the room rise the longer he stood there returning their gazes.

He reached into his back pocket and pulled out a folded piece of paper. Earlier, while LL and uuuuuuU had been getting ready for the bar, Xxxxxxx had pored over his notes, amalgamating all his favourite parts into one final poem he now held in his hands. He unfolded the paper and cleared his throat.

"Sitting on the couch
High as a skyscraper
Playboys and dishes litter the table
The girl on the TV screen is on top of the world
She gets paid in six figures
To choke on his cock as he pulls on her curls
And just like the seed turns into the flower
The consummate dark horse gets paid by the hour
He says 'I'm like a billboard and you're like a highway

You'll act like you're moving
And I'll pretend anybody's buying
That there's no movie star who can hold a light to me
When I put on a smile everyday
I've almost called you eight times this week
To see if you still remember my name
It'll be twelve before the end of the day
So instead, I will lay this bouquet on your grave'"

The audience burst into applause. Xxxxxxx nodded his head slowly in a "thank you" gesture and retreated to the booth where his friends were seated.

"That was AMAZING!" said LL, already tipsy. She threw her arms around Xxxxxxx as he sat next to her and lay her head on his shoulder. Xxxxxxx and uuuuuuU shared a look.

"That was great, Xxxxxxx" said uuuuuuU, "shame there's no money in *that*. They ate you up."

"You really think so?" said Xxxxxxx.

"One hundred percent!" said LL, now sitting upright.

uuuuuuU nodded, then smacked the table with her open palm.

"Alright! Next round's on me!" she exclaimed.

They drank until last call, then crossed the street for some late-night ramen before stumbling back to the apartment.

As LL unlocked the front door, an inebriated uuuuuuU pushed past her confidently, pointing down the hall that led to her bedroom.

"To bed!" she cried. She stood at attention, saluted enthusiastically, turned on her heels, and marched down the hallway. When her bedroom door shut, a muffled "atteeeeen-*tion!*" came from within and LL and Xxxxxx burst into laughter.

"What a kook," said Xxxxxx.

"I love her," said LL.

She walked into the kitchen and grabbed two beers from the fridge.

"Nightcap?" she asked.

Xxxxxx nodded.

"Sure."

She popped the caps off and passed one to Xxxxxx, who then followed her into the living room. She sat down on the couch where he had slept the night before.

Xxxxxx paused in the doorway.

"Oh, are we skipping drinks and going straight to bed?" he joked.

"What—oh!"

LL burst into laughter as Xxxxxx joined her on the couch.

"Good one," she said, "but you're sleeping in there tonight."

She pointed to her bedroom door.

"Oh, am I?" challenged Xxxxxx.

LL's eyes went wide.

"Only if you want to! Sorry, I shouldn't have spoken for you," she backpedaled.

Now it was Xxxxxx's turn to laugh.

"I'm kidding," he said.

He took a swig of his beer.

"I do want to, by the way" he confirmed.

That was all LL needed to hear. She also took a sip of her beer, then straddled Xxxxxx, kissing his neck.

"Whoever cums first gets coffee in the morning?"

"Deal," said Xxxxxx.

They made out on the couch for a while longer before LL took Xxxxxx's hand and led him to her bedroom.

. . . .

"Next."

LL stepped up to the cash at ~~ort~~.

"Two large black coffees, please," said LL.

"Two hangover specials comin' up," said the cashier.

LL chuckled once, then her headache put an end to that nonsense. She shielded her eyes against the daylight streaming in through the windows and got a better look at her cashier. Her memory was foggy, but she looked familiar.

"Hey, have we met?" she asked.

"Doubt it. I just moved here," said the cashier, "Why?"

"You look familiar is all. Where did you move from?"

"Why so many questions?"

"Please. It's going to bother me all day if I can't figure it out."

"7*t*hx*," said the cashier reluctantly.

"That's it!" exclaimed LL, her head throbbing in unison with her excitement at solving the puzzle, "I was just there earlier this week. I think I saw your face on a bus ad or something. What're you doing in 3—-rr/l?"

The cashier pushed her copper hair back behind her ears to get a better look at the woman interrogating her so early in the morning.

"What's your name?" she asked.

"LL," said LL.

"Well, LL," said M, "It's kind of a funny story. Stop me if you've heard it before."

THE END.

About the Author

Stefan Jurewicz is a musician (The Desert Island Big Band), producer (Kick Me Records), and audio engineer living in Ottawa, Canada. Inspired by writers like Charles Bukowski, Kurt Vonnegut, and William Burroughs, Jurewicz's writing is a constant turf war between lighthearted wit and misanthropic candor, as silly as it is visceral.

Read more at desertislandbigband.com.